CONFESSIONS & PAYBACK
ON A VOLGA CRUISE

CONFESSIONS & PAYBACK
ON A VOLGA CRUISE

JONATHAN HYDE

iUniverse, Inc.
Bloomington

CONFESSIONS & PAYBACK ON A VOLGA CRUISE

iUniverse books may be ordered through booksellers or by contacting:

iUniverse
1663 Liberty Drive
Bloomington, IN 47403
www.iuniverse.com
1-800-Authors (1-800-288-4677)

ISBN: 978-1-4759-4814-1 (sc)
ISBN: 978-1-4759-4815-8 (ebk)

Library of Congress Control Number: 2012916332

Printed in the United States of America

iUniverse rev. date: 09/05/2012

"Everyone has something to confess."
The Closer, TV

"If you live to seek revenge,
Dig a grave for two."
Ancient Jewish Proverb

"Revenge, at first so sweet,
Bitter ere long back on itself recoils."
John Milton, *Paradise Lost*, book IX, line 171

"To exact revenge for yourself
and your friends is not only a right,
It's an absolute duty."
Stieg Larsson

FOR

Sasha & Asya

Friends *extraordinaires*

PROLOGUE

The Volga is the longest river in Europe, meandering three thousand miles through locks, lakes, and other waterways enabling passage from St. Petersburg on the Baltic Sea to Astrakhan on the Caspian Sea. It is a magnet for tourism. On a warm, sunny day sailboats with colorful spinnakers dot the horizon. There are motorboats, too, darting around cruise ships taking tourists for weekend trips, often to an uninhabited island for hiking and mushroom picking. Tourists with time and money on their hands, particularly foreigners, can be wined and dined for ten days on luxury liners that ply the waters between Moscow and St. Petersburg or Moscow and Astrakhan. It was at Moscow's Northern Port that the *Novikov Priboi* awaited the arrival of its passengers for a September cruise to St. Petersburg sponsored by two American university alumni associations.

The arrivals would include three couples with very little in common, except for the fact that the husbands all had something less than noble in their pasts. By the end of the voyage, two of the husbands would regret that they hadn't heeded the words on a memento from the Soviet past which was for sale in the ship's souvenir shop. "*Watch What You Say!*" was the caption under the image of a grim young woman with a red bandanna around her head and the forefinger of her right hand to her lips. The memento was available as a poster, a pin, or a refrigerator magnet.

Like most of the passengers, the three couples flew into Moscow's Sheremet'evo airport and were transported by bus to the ship. All three were on the Delta daily flight from JFK with first class tickets. They would dine together aboard the *Novikov Priboi*, and a certain amount of intimacy would develop between the Oglebys, the Pickles, and the Krukases.

Neville Ogleby was a retired Foreign Service Officer, having attained the rank of ambassador to one of the ten poorest African nations. Upon retirement he was hired by a New York university as an administrator and fund raiser. He also shared his experiences and knowledge about international affairs with undergraduate students. The department of political science voted against a professorial rank, which embittered Ogleby, but the university provost gave him the rank of a professor of practice. In accepting a teaching position, Ogleby insisted that he be permitted to teach a course on ethics and international relations, although ethics was not his strong point, as time would tell.

A graduate of a prestigious New England preparatory school as well as Harvard University, Neville felt entitled. Even in his seventies he had an air about him, and he still thought that he could charm the pants off the opposite sex. He was no longer the squash player that he had once been, and he had begun to shuffle. But he was still married to Moody, whose reaction to Neville's flirtations was to imitate the hair style of Jackie Kennedy. In other respects, however, Moody was nondescript, even a bit frumpy. Her life revolved around Neville and their two children, although she had laughed when Neville showed her a newspaper article that suggested sex every day for a year might reinvigorate their marriage. As an alternative, Moody suggested a cruise on the Volga.

Unlike the Oglebys, the Pickles were not pretentious. Francis was a child psychologist whose costly divorce had been quickly followed by marriage to a wealthy widow seven years his senior. They had met at an attorney's office, where Blanche was discussing her late husband's will and Francis his bankruptcy proceedings. Francis was struck first by Blanche's Botox beauty and then by her bank account. Blanche, whose education ended after two years at a community college, was flattered that a younger man with a doctorate could find her desirable. The Volga cruise was Blanche's wedding gift to Francis, whose travels rarely took him outside New York State, where he was born, raised, educated, and had a private practice.

Blanche's gift had been inspired by a chance-meeting with Moody Ogleby, who worked as a volunteer in the sales gallery at a local museum known nationally for its collection of ceramic pieces. When Blanche told Moody that she was looking for something unique, something for a special occasion, Moody laughed and suggested a cruise on the Volga instead of a bowl with a crystalline glaze. Moody took an INTRAV brochure from her purse and gave it to Blanche, who soon became more interested in the Volga than in ceramics. Two months later the Pickles were sitting across the aisle from the Oglebys on the flight to Moscow.

Peter Krukas, like Francis Pickle, was also divorced, but with no hard feelings. He and his first wife had simply drifted apart after twenty-six years of marriage. Peter's parents were Lithuanian, and Petras, as his parents preferred to call him, had been raised with two languages and two cultures. As a young man he had been a star lacrosse player, and as an adult he was an avid skier. In short, he was physically fit and didn't look his age. Most striking at first glance were his eyes—two amber marbles with blue flakes. Peter took in stride jokes about his having the eyes of an Australian shepherd born with the merle gene.

From early on Peter had an eye for art, a passion that led to his establishing a prominent art gallery in New York City. Like his stunning wife Madge, whose short curly hair with streaks of gray suited the pince-nez that she wore when reading, Peter was eager to see the icons and paintings in Russian museums, most notably the Tretyakovsky Gallery in Moscow and the Hermitage in St. Petersburg. Madge, a prominent realtor, also wanted to get a firsthand look at the booming real estate market in Russia, a recent phenomenon made possible by the collapse of the Soviet Union and the advent of what Russians called wild capitalism under President Boris Yeltsin.

The first busload of passengers, which included the three couples, was guided up a gangplank and across the deck of the *Lenin* to a parallel ship, the *Novikov Priboi*, where they were welcomed by the tour director, a middle-aged Russian woman, pleasingly plump with an infectious smile, and by the tour study leader, a tall lanky retired American professor with gray hair, bushy eyebrows, and almond shaped eyes. They, too, had confessions to make, at least to each other.

Zhanna Mikhailovna graduated from Moscow State University (MGU) with a degree in foreign languages, which led immediately to a job with the Russian Travel Agency *Intourist* during the Brezhnev era. It was at the Intourist Hotel, a stone's throw from the Kremlin, that she had first met John Lockerbie, already a veteran traveler to the Soviet Union. As an *Intourist* representative, Zhanna was the one who gave John the requisite coupons for breakfast, lunch, and dinner. He had used a coupon for tea to get acquainted with Zhanna. With the passage of time, which included John's divorce and his decision to buy an apartment in Moscow, John and Zhanna became colleagues on cruise ships and friends at home. Home included Zhanna's father, Viktor, with whom John developed a close relationship. John considered Viktor a steadfast friend and devoted father, but he knew that Viktor was intolerant of lies and deception and could become an avenging angel.

Like Zhanna, John was outgoing and excited when talking about Russia. With three degrees in Soviet studies, he had entered academia in 1963. Some administrators took umbrage at his willingness to speak out on controversial matters. But undergraduates loved him. In an annual course critique, one undergraduate wrote that students in his courses wished he could teach every class at the university. Upon retirement, John jumped at the chance to be a study leader on Russian cruise ships along the Volga. After his first cruise, John received a letter from the sponsors saying that he had received rave reviews not only from the passengers but also from Zhanna, who had moved up the Intourist ladder from interpreter in a hotel, since demolished, to cruise director on luxury ships.

"Every trip is an adventure," Zhanna said to John as they headed down to the bar for a libation after greeting the last of the passengers to board the *Novikov Priboi*.

CHAPTER 1

T he welcome aboard dinner was a sumptuous buffet catered by waitresses in short, formfitting black skirts and sleeveless white blouses. The attractive young women poured vodka and champagne like water. Moody Ogleby nudged her husband forward, whispering that he would see the black derrières at other meals but that this might be his last chance to fill his plate with caviar, wild game, and sterlets in a champagne sauce.

Peter Krukas, standing behind Moody, put the gourmet treats into context. "Tell Neville that Stalin served Winston Churchill the same delicacies during their discussions in the Kremlin about a Second Front in Europe." Peter continued with a chuckle. "My Lithuanian parents told me that it was the same printed menu, along with a few misspellings, that was handed to General Sikorksi in December 1941 when he visited Moscow as Head of the Polish Provisional Government."

Balancing glasses of champagne with the cornucopia on their plates, the Oglebys and Krukases headed for an empty table. Moody noticed the Pickles looking for a spot. She waved to them and pointed to empty seats at their table. "Come join us," Moody and Neville shouted in unison, causing other passengers to look in their direction. John, too, decided to answer the call.

After greetings and small talk about points of origin, seven glasses of champagne were raised in a toast. "*Na zdorove!* To your health!" John said. "As your study leader on this trip," he added after savoring pellets of black caviar and slivers of ice cold sturgeon, "I would be interested in any first impressions that you may have of Russia."

"My god, the traffic!" Blanche exclaimed, raising a hand with carefully manicured nails as if in surrender.

"It's worse than in New York City," Madge added. "It took almost an hour to get from the airport to the ship. Bumper to bumper for what, ten miles?"

"I thought that Russia was a communist country," Francis chimed in, "with no private ownership of automobiles."

"I'll give you a little history," John said. "The big break for individuals came under Brezhnev, who was notorious for his love of fast cars. He invested a huge amount of money in the Volga Motor Vehicle Plant, which was designed by the Italian Company Fiat to produce 600,000 cars every year. When Brezhnev came to power in 1964 there were only a million cars in all of the Soviet Union."

"Isn't that the factory that Prime Minister Putin recently visited?" Blanche asked. "The clip on American television was hilarious."

"I didn't think that Putin could generate a laugh," Neville said.

"It wasn't on purpose," Blanche responded. "He got into one of the cars as a pitch for domestic automobiles. TV cameras were rolling. When Putin turned the key, several times, the car wouldn't start!"

"In point of fact, the Zhiguli is not a bad car," John commented. "But after Yeltsin stepped down as President in 1999, the Russian market was flooded with foreign cars. When you came in from the airport you may have noticed the billboards featuring Audis, Volvos, BMWs, Land-Rovers, the Lexus RX350, Jaguars, Ferraris, and Bentleys."

"All that I noticed," Francis said, "were the bottlenecks."

"You can't avoid them," John replied, "Last month President Medvedev condemned what he called Moscow's notorious traffic jams. One Wednesday evening they stretched almost 3,000 kilometers according to *Yandex.Probki*, which monitors the traffic situation in Moscow. The road from Sheremet'evo airport, which you all experienced, is the very worst."

"Why's that?" Peter asked.

"Not just because it's a major artery," John answered. "There is constant construction on the highway, sometimes stalled because of squabbles between state and city authorities. And right now there's another factor, too. A second airport, Vnukovo, has been closed for runway repairs, which means that Russian officials and foreign delegations are now flying out of Sheremet'evo. When they travel to and from the airport, the highway is temporarily closed to other vehicles."

"What a mess," Madge said, shaking her head. "I guess things will get better when construction comes to an end."

"No one here believes that," John said. "Not even President Medvedev. He has ordered the government to stagger working hours for employees of state and federal agencies. That might ease, but not solve, Moscow's traffic problems. The problem is too many cars."

"Do you have one, John?" Blanche asked.

"Yes, but I rarely use it. It's faster to get around the city with public transportation. And it's almost impossible to find a parking spot, which explains why so many cars are up on sidewalks."

"Don't the police issue tickets?" Francis asked.

"Ah, the road police, the *gaishniki*." John smiled.

"What's so funny?" Francis asked.

"The *gaishniki* are looking for bigger fish to fry."

"What does that mean?" Moody asked.

"In a recent poll, 52% of the respondents put the road police in first place for corruption. Bribes that are solicited or offered are usually paid on the spot to inspectors. Big money comes not from small infractions, such as failing to buckle up, but from speeding and driving under the influence."

"I read in *Forbes* magazine," Peter commented, "that Russia has the worst road-fatalities record in Europe: 35,000 deaths and 300,000 injuries every year. The article cited speed and alcohol as the primary causes."

"Don't drivers ever complain about extortion?" Blanche asked.

"The article in *Forbes*," Peter answered, "said that most Russians feel it would be a waste of time."

"All sorts of suggestions and proposals have been made to reduce corruption by the *gaishniki*," John said. "Pay money directly to the State Bank. Purchase a debit card designed exclusively for traffic violations. Use a newly established 24-hour telephone hotline to report corruption. Or, more promising, increase wages for traffic cops so that they are not so dependent on money offered to them or demanded by them."

"Have you ever had a run-in with the police?" Francis asked.

"Once. I was chased and stopped for failing to pull over when a cop raised his baton. He wanted to see my papers. I had a ten-dollar bill in my passport as a precaution. To my amazement, the money was still in my passport when my documents were returned. But the experience made me want to drive an extra mile to avoid police checkpoints."

"When I was teaching at the university," Neville said, "a Russian émigré in the School of Music was stopped for speeding on the New York Thruway. In line with what you describe as Russian mores on the highway, he tried to bribe the state trooper. The professor learned the hard way."

Francis smiled. "Bribes don't always work."

"It wasn't a bribe that saved my Subaru," John said, capturing the attention of his dinner companions. "A neighbor upstairs called the police when she saw two guys breaking into my car. If they had gotten away with it, I might have been out of luck."

"Why's that?" Madge asked.

"If a Moscow driver is found in possession of a car stolen from the West, the traffic cop will issue a one-year permit. If no one claims the car within a year, it becomes 'naturalized.' I was told by one officer that Westerners are rich enough to afford a new car if the old one is stolen."

"You don't have a garage?" Madge continued, thinking of her own Volvo.

"I could buy a steel cage or a metal box, like some of my neighbors, but I prefer to park my car on the narrow road in front of my building."

"Even in winter?"

"Sure, night and day. I rarely move it, except when there were terrorist bombings a few years ago. At that time cars couldn't be parked in the same spot for more than twenty-four hours. Now we are concerned with burglars, not terrorists."

"On the drive in from the airport," Blanche said, "I was struck by the construction of new apartment buildings. Are they like yours?"

"I moved into a high-rise a few years ago when my *Khrushchevka* was torn down by the city."

"What's a *Khrushchevka*?" Madge the inquisitive, driven, and successful real estate broker asked.

"They are five-story apartment buildings constructed during the Khrushchev era to alleviate the housing shortage. Until 1991 they were all owned by the state. Then came privatization."

"What's privatization?" Madge continued.

"It's a program instituted in Russia by President Boris Yeltsin when the Soviet Union collapsed. The first phase was the printing of 10,000-ruble privatization checks given to Russian citizens. They were supposed to facilitate private investment in enterprises. It didn't work. The privatization tsar, Anatolii Chubais, would later admit that the people got nothing from their vouchers. What they did get from privatization, however, was the right to become owners of their state apartments."

"Did it cost a lot to buy an apartment?" Francis asked.

"Next to nothing. Only a modest registration fee."

"I would have been first in line to buy my apartment," Madge joked.

"Russians were slow to hop on the bandwagon," John responded. "Many thought it was a trick with hidden costs. By now, however, most apartments have been privatized. That means an owner can live in the apartment, rent it, or sell it. A Russian sold me his apartment fifteen years ago."

"Why was your building torn down?" Peter asked.

"The *Khrushchevki* were thought of by the government as a temporary solution to the housing problem. Take a look at one here in Moscow, and you'll understand why the government has decided to replace them with high-rise apartment buildings. Also, it's a better utilization of space for the city's burgeoning population."

"What happens to people living in a *Khrushchevka* when it's torn down?" Madge asked.

"That depends," John said.

"On what?"

"If you don't own your apartment, the city will move you to a new complex, usually south of the city's ring road. Not a great location for public transportation. If you own your apartment, it's a bit more complicated. You are given several months notice prior to demolition of the building, and by law you should be given a new home in the same district. That would mean waiting for construction of a new building. As an alternative, the city offers housing in three locations outside of your district."

"What did you do?" Francis asked. "I would have demanded monetary compensation. I would have thought about a bribe, too."

"A bribe would have helped, but I played by the rules. I rejected the three locations offered by the city, insisting on an apartment in my own district. Unlike Russian friends with the same problem, I could wait for a new building. I lived in my American home while the new building was being constructed."

"Was it worth waiting for?" Neville asked, thinking about some of the crummy places he had resided in while a Foreign Service Officer in Africa. Could Moscow be any different?

"On the negative side, I'm on the twelfth floor. The building is not neighbor friendly, unlike my *Khrushchevka* apartment where we knew and helped each other."

"Like apartment buildings today in New York City," Madge commented. "We nod to neighbors in the lobby. That's it. But we love our place."

"I love mine, too," John said. "As the old saying goes, don't let the negative eliminate the positive."

"What's positive?" Neville asked, reflecting his negative view of America's Cold War enemy.

"First of all, it's new, bigger, and didn't cost me a penny."

"Just rubles," Peter joked.

"No charge at all for my new home. I made a bundle."

"How so?" Francis asked, wishing that he too could make a bundle someday. He didn't want to go bankrupt again.

"I bought my first apartment for $28,000. My new one is worth close to $300,000. If I were to sell the place, I would be rolling in clover. At the moment, I plan to keep both my Russian apartment and my house in the States. I go back and forth."

"Do you rent your apartment when you're in the States?" Madge asked. "If it's like an apartment in Manhattan, you'd make a small fortune."

"I would get about $1,000 a month, but I like to come and go as I please."

"What about your monthly expenses?" Francis asked.

"They are minimal. Less than $100 a month for everything. The biggest monthly expense for everyone is a housing fee (*kvartplata*). Mine is the equivalent of eighty-five dollars, somewhat lower than what other residents pay because I live alone. A sign outside our neighborhood housing office indicates that many Russians are already having a hard time making their *kvartplata* payments."

"What's the sign say?" Blanche asked.

"Something like, 'You may think that Russian courts are the most humane in the world, but guess again if you don't pay your *kvartplata*.' And it's getting worse rather than better. The *kvartplata* is expected to go up by 15% this year."

"Maybe you'll end up selling your apartment," Madge commented.

"I'll give the idea a second thought in three or four years when the government puts in place a property tax based on the market value of your home."

"If you need a realtor, I'm at your service."

"You'd make good money, Madge. Buyers continue to line up in spite of the financial crisis here and abroad."

"Where do they get the money?" Moody asked.

"Not from their salaries. The average Moscow wage is about $1,500 a month."

"Mortgages?" Madge asked.

"That's the answer. A down payment, reduced from 30% to 20%, on a thirty-year mortgage with a fixed rate of 14% for dollars and 18% for rubles. Prime Minister Putin wants the rate lowered to 11% for dollars."

"That's highway robbery," Francis chimed in. "Aren't there defaults, like in the United States?"

"Yes, it's a real problem. The average monthly mortgage payment is at least half the average monthly salary received by the middle class. To live comfortably, Muscovites say that their income needs to go up by 40%."

"Now that I think about it," Madge laughed, "I don't want to be your realtor. I have enough headaches in Manhattan."

"Is your apartment safe?" Peter asked. "We have a concierge."

"There's a concierge in our building, too. She provides some security. I also have a steel door. But nothing is foolproof."

"Does that mean you've been burglarized?" Neville asked.

"Once. When I came home from a trip to Lithuania, my door was ajar. The place had been trashed. My computer was gone, but the burglar missed five hundred dollars that I had hidden in my shaving kit." Remembering his small triumph, John smiled.

"What did the police say?" Moody asked.

"The first thing they said was that even a steel door is not a challenge. It's a specialty of burglars from the Caucasus. If you have what is called a 'signalization' system connected to police headquarters, the police guarantee that the burglar will either be caught or will be scared off from the scene before completion of his criminal act."

"I gather you don't have such a system," Madge said. "Does that mean your burglar got away with it?"

"Yes and no. After other successful burglaries in the neighborhood, he was tripped up by *signalizatsiia*. The police caught the unemployed migrant from Georgia red-handed. He confessed to everything, even to the fact that he found a cache of dollars not in my apartment but in the apartment of a Russian teacher. Other stuff he either sent home or sold at a nearby railroad station. The police transcript, which I got after the trial, is a better read than a good mystery novel."

John's colloquy ended when Zhanna tapped her microphone for an announcement. "I just want to remind all of you that buses will be waiting tomorrow morning at 9:00 a.m. sharp for your tour of the Kremlin, Red Square, St. Basil's cathedral, and GUM."

"What's GUM?" Moody asked, turning to John.

"It's the landmark department store on Red Square. With money you can buy any luxury good that's available in the West. It's no longer the old stodgy store that it was in the Soviet era. A striking indication of change can be found on the ground floor in *Gastronom No. 1*, a gourmet food store stocked with every conceivable staple and delicacy, both foreign and domestic."

"Do you shop there?" Neville asked.

"Hardly ever. I like my neighborhood chain store, *Perekrëstok*."

"Less expensive?" Francis asked.

"Absolutely, but not dirt cheap. Prime Minister Putin recently charged the mother company with price gouging."

"Will you be with us tomorrow morning?" Blanche asked.

"No, but I have a question. Can I interest anyone in a visit to a cemetery after the Kremlin tour?"

"Are we going to be that tired?" Peter asked, with a smile on his face.

"I guarantee that you'll be thrilled, not interred. If any of you are interested, Zhanna will deliver you to me at noon next to your bus behind St. Basil's. I'll be waiting for any takers."

CHAPTER 2

J ohn shaded his eyes from the bright noon sun, walking briskly up an incline to the back of St. Basil's where tourist buses waited for their charges. It was easy to spot Zhanna. Smiling as usual, she was caught up in animated conversation with a small group of familiar faces. When John reached her, they gave each other friendly hugs.

"These are the hardy souls who want to continue walking rather than return to the ship for an afternoon siesta," Zhanna said. "They're all yours. Don't lose them!"

"Don't worry. I won't let them out of my sight."

"The metro will pose a challenge," Zhanna warned. "It's usually packed at this time of day."

"We need to stay together as we get on and off the train. Anyone want to help?"

"I'll be an usher," Peter volunteered. "I'm used to crowded subways."

"The similarity ends there," John said. "Moscow's metro system is beautiful as well as efficient."

"Isn't there a metro tour scheduled for tomorrow?" Blanche asked.

"Good point," John said. "You'll be taken in small groups in the afternoon to see stations with mosaics, stained glass murals, carvings, and bronze statues. They are works of art. One of my favorites is the newest station, the *Dostoevsky* station, depicting stark scenes in black and white from his novel *Crime and Punishment*."

"Will we see it on our way to the cemetery?" Moody asked.

"It's not on our metro line, the red line," John answered. "We're not going very far. Only five stops. Again, a word of caution. Stay together getting on and off the train. Be pushy if necessary to make sure that we stay together as a group. Okay?"

"Got it," Peter the volunteer said with authority and a grin.

With his sergeant-at-arms at his side, John led the group up to the Kremlin and across the cobblestones of Red Square to a shopping mall, *Okhotnyi Ryad*, built under what used to be an open square noted for its parades and demonstrations. Along with chic Western stores, the mall also has an entrance to the metro's red line.

"This way," John said as he led the group down stairs and along corridors to turnstiles for the red line. "We'll go through using my card, one by one starting with Peter. Wait for the red light to turn green."

"A train's coming," Neville said, itching to pick up speed.

"There's no rush. Trains come every two or three minutes. See those orange numbers up there in front of the train as it pulls in? They tell you the interval between arrivals."

"Why, then, are some people running?" Madge asked.

"Human nature, perhaps," Francis the psychologist offered.

"Let's cluster together as we get on," John said. "Don't go for a seat unless it's close to the door. It's only five stops. When the doors open, out we go. Quickly."

At their destination, *Sportivnaia*, Peter and John got the group off with a few shoves, making sure that no one was pushed back by rowdy soccer fans returning from the Lenin Sports Stadium.

"So far, so good," John said to Peter as the group went by escalator up to a street that was filled with vendors hawking their wares. "It's only a ten-minute walk to the Novodevichy cemetery."

When they reached the red brick entrance, John motioned to the group to stop. "Before we go in, I want to give you some background about this burial place, which is second only to burial in the Kremlin Wall. Frankly, I would prefer to be here. It's fascinating, peaceful, and beautiful. The serenity is broken only by church bells from the adjacent convent and by the cawing of an occasional crow overhead."

"Sounds like you might want to be buried here," Peter commented.

"I don't have the connections."

"Wouldn't a bribe help?" Francis asked.

"Maybe today, but not in the Soviet period. The director of the cemetery during the Brezhnev years stated in a recent interview that applications for a burial plot had to be signed by two members of the Communist Party's Politburo. In order to prevent bribery, 'clients' (*klienty*) were assigned gravesites in the order in which applications were received. Choice was not an option."

"But the cemetery is open to all visitors?" Moody asked.

"Today, yes. Not so in the Brezhnev era. When I got to the gate in the late 1970s, it was closed. I asked a policeman standing at the entrance if the cemetery would be open later in the day. He almost laughed, stating that the cemetery had been closed to tourists for seven years."

"Why was it closed?" Moody continued.

"Until recently I thought it was because Brezhnev didn't want admirers of Khrushchev to visit his gravesite. Brezhnev wanted to put an end to Khrushchev's de-Stalinization campaign, launched in 1956 at a party congress. I'll say more about this when we visit Khrushchev's grave."

"You think differently now?" Peter asked.

"Not really, but it's possible that Politburo member Viktor Grishin, exercising his authority as head of the Moscow party apparatus, put the nix on easy access to the cemetery."

"Why would he do that?" Neville asked.

"Rumor has it that Grishin was upset by old ladies running around the hallowed grounds shouting and waving shopping bags."

"Shopping bags?" Madge asked quizzically.

"Times were tough," John said. "Russians were pouring into Moscow from outlying areas to buy food. In their spare time these aunts with shopping bags (*tetki s sumkami*), as they were called, would roam through the cemetery as part of their group's so-called cultural program."

"Are we going to get culture, too?" Blanche asked.

"You bet," John answered, leading the group through the main gate. "Let's start with Boris Yeltsin's gravesite. It's straight ahead, over to your left."

"You mean that red, blue, and white sarcophagus?" Madge asked. "It's ugly."

"I agree," John said. "It stands out like a sore thumb."

"None of the tourists ahead of us seem interested in his grave," Moody remarked.

"Not even right after his burial," John said. "I came to the cemetery the day after his interment. I thought the grounds might be closed to prevent an influx of tourists and well-wishers. I was wrong. When I got to the grotesque stone marker, shaped and colored like the Russian flag, I was alone."

"I thought Russians loved Yeltsin. Americans did," Neville said. "President Clinton described Yeltsin as a patriot who defended peace, freedom, and progress."

"Many Russians would disagree," John said. "Some see Yeltsin as a genetic dictator. His former press secretary described Yeltsin as a man for whom power was his ideology, his friend, his concubine, his mistress, and his passion."

"Those are strong words," Peter commented.

"Yes, but don't forget 1993," John explained. "President Yeltsin ordered tanks to fire on the Russian White House, which was controlled by opposition forces led by the Vice-President and the Speaker of Parliament. Over a hundred lives were lost. Even Yeltsin loyalists admit that he made unpopular decisions in an undemocratic way."

After a moment of silence, not reverence, John led the group to one of his favorite gravesites.

"This is the memorial to Gorbachev's wife, Raisa Maksimovna. The statue is elegant, at least in my eyes, and there are always flowers at the base. As you can see, it's a corner plot. The red brick walls meeting at the corner behind the grave contain ashes of less prominent people."

"Didn't Yeltsin rescue Gorbachev during an unsuccessful coup against the Soviet President?" Neville asked.

"After talking on the telephone with a leader of the putsch, Yeltsin sent a team to free Gorbachev from his *dacha* on the Crimean peninsula. The team was led by Vice-President Rutskoi, accompanied by the Russian Prime Minister. They flew to Foros with troops from the Ryazan Officers' School."

"Gorbachev must have been thankful," Neville said.

"In one sense, yes, but there was a mutual dislike between the two men. When Gorbachev was in power, the Communist Party stripped Yeltsin of his party duties at the local and national level. Yeltsin's subsequent request for political rehabilitation was turned down."

"That would be enough to make anyone mad," Neville said, remembering how he had been turned down for a regular professorial rank at his university. "I guess Yeltsin was not a vengeful person."

"On the contrary," John corrected. "He had a history of vengeance and vindictiveness rather than magnanimity. He admits in his memoirs that he went tooth and nail for his homeroom teacher in primary school. As for Gorbachev, Yeltsin couldn't resist badgering and lecturing him at a meeting of the Russian Supreme Soviet soon after Gorbachev's return to Moscow from house arrest in the Crimea. More on Yeltsin's temperament when we get to our next site."

John led the group to a massive statue of a Russian general bedecked with medals and seated next to a sword and shield. "That's Aleksandr Ivanovich Lebed. In 1995 he gave up a military career for politics."

"Looks like he didn't make it," Francis remarked snidely.

"That's not entirely true," John replied. "At the end of the year he was elected to the Russian State Duma. In 1996, in the first round of the presidential election, he came in third with 14.5% of the popular vote. Yeltsin was the front-runner. In order to ensure victory in the runoff election, Yeltsin bought Lebed's support by appointing him Secretary of the Security Council of the Russian Federation."

"Sounds like a good deal to me," Francis said.

"Short-lived," John said. "A few months after the second round of voting, President Yeltsin dismissed Lebed from his newly acquired post. It was a dramatic appearance on national television."

"What caused his removal?" Madge asked.

"Western businessmen interpreted it as a signal that the struggle against crime and corruption in Russia was a lost cause. In an interview with British journalists, Lebed had charged that half the country consisted of criminals and the other half were police in pursuit of criminals. That sort of talk wasn't what Yeltsin wanted to hear."

"Was Lebed always outspoken?" Neville asked.

"Nothing was off limits to him. He once said that the government keeps the doughnut and gives the people only the hole. Lebed also told a journalist that most Russians don't care whether they are ruled by fascists or communists or even martians so long as they can buy six kinds of sausage and lots of cheap vodka."

"But somebody must like him," Moody interjected. "There are flowers at the base of his memorial."

"You'll see flowers at our next stop, too," John said, directing the group over to a parallel path that led up to the grave of Nikita S. Khrushchev.

"It's unusual," Madge said as she looked up at Khrushchev's bronze face surrounded by slabs of black and white marble. Like her husband, Madge appreciated audacity in art.

"There's a story behind the memorial," John responded. "It was crafted for the family by a dissident artist whose work had been condemned by Khrushchev."

"Khrushchev didn't like Stalin either," Neville said in a professorial voice.

"You're right, of course," John acknowledged. "In 1956 at the Twentieth Party Congress Khrushchev attacked Stalin for committing crimes against the party and crimes against the nation. It was a bold and unexpected move, causing some delegates to gasp and even faint. As Gorbachev would later say, Khrushchev was a man of courage."

"I guess Brezhnev disagreed," Neville continued. "That's why Khrushchev was removed from power in 1964."

"It's a bit more complicated than that, Neville."

"Okay. Let's skip it. What's next?"

"There are dozens of famous people buried here from all walks of life. In addition to politicians and military figures, the cemetery is the final resting place for composers, artists, actors, scholars, diplomats, and literary luminaries like Gogol, Chekhov, and Bulgakov. What I'm going to do is to walk you quickly through the rest of the cemetery pointing out my favorite gravestones. You'll recognize some if not all of the names."

As they moved into the oldest sections of the cemetery they paused to admire three monuments on their right. A ballerina in relief on a towering slab of white alabaster. A clown with his pet dog, both in bronze. And the more recent grave of the master choreographer of folk dances, Igor Moiseev, whose photograph was still in place in front of a large wooden cross.

The group moved on to grave #9 in section #4. It was a huge white marble statue of a man reposing in a chair. "That's Fedor Shaliapin, the world famous bass. One can imagine him contemplating his last aria in the Mariinsky Theater."

After passing the lifelike image of a Soviet cosmonaut inside a ring of metal with flight helmet in hand, John paused. He pointed to a cross carved from a massive piece of dark brown wood. "On your tour of the Kremlin this morning, Zhanna no doubt told you that the ashes of two Americans, John Reed and Big Bill Hayward, are buried in the Kremlin Wall. There's an American here, too. Michael Rayback. He was a close friend of Zhanna's father."

Neville seemed taken aback. "He was department chair at my university. How did he get here?"

"It's a long story," John said. "To be brief, Rayback moved to Russia after a bitter divorce. The love of his life over here was the daughter of KGB General Anatolii Semenov, Hero of the Soviet Union. His ashes and those of Michael Rayback are buried on the other side of that wooden cross, beneath symbols of the security police."

Moody looked at Neville. "A ghost from the past," she whispered, recalling her husband's animosity toward the man who had been his boss for five years.

Staring off into space, Neville changed the subject. "What's next?"

"Up ahead is the dark and brooding bust of the revolutionary poet Vladimir Mayakovsky," John said.

"It's breathtaking, set against that bloodred marble backdrop," Peter said as the group moved to the front of the monument.

"He was only thirty-seven when he died," John said.

"What did he die of?" Moody asked.

"Suicide," John answered. "Many believe that he had become disillusioned with communism. The same could be said of Nadezhda Sergeevna Allilueva."

"Who's she?" Neville asked.

"Stalin's second wife," John said, leading the group to grave #1 in section #1.

"What's wrong with her nose?" Neville asked, staring at a facial image of Nadezhda Sergeevna chiseled in white and enclosed in Plexiglass.

"Soon after her burial, vandals broke the nose on the memorial. It was repaired and is now protected. But the color of the nose is not exactly the same."

"What did she die of?" Moody asked.

"Like Mayakovsky, she committed suicide. She shot herself."

"Why would she do that?"

"Some say that she had just argued with Stalin about his philandering. Others attribute the suicide to bipolar depression, or to remorse over starvation in Ukraine caused by Stalin's policies."

"There's yet another theory," Peter added. "A few years ago Madge and I saw a documentary film in Greenwich Village at the Quad Theater. It was called 'Stalin's Wife' and was produced by a Russian émigré. The producer rejects suicide as the cause of death. He believes that she was murdered by Stalin."

"Murder, not a suicide," Neville repeated slowly and with some agitation, recalling a three-way conversation in his past about the death of Rayback's first wife.

"Are you all right?" Moody asked.

"Sure." Neville smiled. "Only hunger pangs."

Seizing the moment, John suggested that the group might like to end the afternoon with a meal at a Georgian restaurant, *U Pirosmani*, right around the corner.

"Just what the doctor ordered!" Neville said, almost relieved.

"The restaurant is named in honor of a renowned Georgian artist, Niko Pirosmanishvili," John said.

"Will we see some of his paintings?" Peter asked. "Maybe I could buy one for my art gallery."

"Like President Clinton, who dined here in 1996, you will see only reproductions. The owner will probably show us his favorites after we eat what President Clinton described in the guest book as 'a good meal.' Actually, the food will be better than good. You won't forget it."

Outside the cemetery, John turned left and led the group around the walls of the Novodevichy convent to a wooden building located on a neighboring street.

"What a view!" Peter exclaimed as he turned on the steps of the restaurant, looking back across the street at golden domes above a small pond that glistened in the afternoon sun.

At the top of stairs leading to the dining areas, the group was greeted by a hostess who escorted them to a long table by one of the windows. "This is Ilya," she said, introducing their waiter. "He speaks only a little English, but the menu is in English as well as Russian."

Minutes after taking their seats, Ilya brought to the table six bottles of Georgian wine. Three red and three white. Pointing to a bottle of red, Ilya grinned. "Was Stalin favorite. You Americans say 'enjoy.' Pirosmani says *Long live red sun and green grass.*"

When Ilya returned to take their order, John was ready. "We've decided to let you choose for us. Our only request is that they be classic Georgian dishes."

The meal lasted nearly two hours. Georgian bread (lavash and khachapuri) served with a cold starter (red beet salad with walnuts and spices) as well as a hot starter (mutton stewed in white wine with a plum sauce).

"What's next?" Peter asked, licking his lips in anticipation of the main course, which turned out to be lamb shish kebab cooked in wine and cognac for meat eaters, grilled shish kebab from sturgeon for fish lovers, or, for vegetarians, a shish kebab of aubergines, red peppers, and tomatoes cooked over an open fire.

"For dessert," Ilya said at the end of the feast, "me bring pelamushi. Look here on menu."

"A Georgian national dessert from the Kakhetia region, with grape juice, raisins, and walnuts," Blanche said, reading from the menu with interest. She loved to entertain and was always on the lookout for a new recipe.

When the bill came, no one was surprised. It was substantial. Peter said he would put it on his credit card and collect from everyone back on the ship. When Peter handed Ilya his Master card, Ilya shook his head. "Sorry, card no. Only rubles."

John was surprised. "I guess it's a spinoff from the financial crisis. Let's pool our rubles." When they fell short of what was needed, John turned to Ilya. "How about dollars?"

When Ilya returned from a conversation with the owner, he had good news. "Boss say okay."

Ilya got a good tip, in dollars, when the group exited *U Pirosmani* after a look at the art work and a much needed visit to the *tualet*.

"I'm stuffed," Francis said on the sidewalk outside the restaurant.

"I'm tired," Blanche added. "Could we take a taxi back to the ship?"

"We might find taxis at the metro station," John said, "but it would be expensive and would take longer."

The group decided to walk back to the *Sportivnaia* station, where they caught the red line into the center of the city and then the green line up to *Rechnoi vokzal*.

"From here to the ship it's only a ten-minute walk," John said, shepherding his flock from *Rechnoi vokzal* through an adjacent park to the Moscow River.

"Home again," Francis said, pointing to the *Novikov Priboi*.

"Rest up," John said. "Tomorrow will be another busy day. In the morning Zhanna will accompany you by bus to the Tretyakovsky Art Gallery."

CHAPTER 3

Z hanna was about to get on the bus with her tourists from the *Novikov Priboi* when John arrived at a trot.

"I thought you were going to meet us at the Gallery," Zhanna said.

"Business at the district office didn't take as long as I thought it would."

"Behind with your housing payments?" Zhanna asked with a smile and a wink.

"Actually, I got money back. The unexpected hike in my *kvartplata* was a mistake on their part. They thought that my apartment in Moscow was a second home in Russia. I wanted to resolve the problem before our cruise begins tomorrow morning."

John took a seat behind the bus driver, and Zhanna tested her microphone.

"Before we reach the Gallery," she announced, "I want to give you folks some background. The Gallery that we will be visiting was founded by a Russian merchant, Paul Tretyakov. He started to collect art when he was a young man, and at the end of the 19th century he donated some two thousand works from his private collection to the city of Moscow. In addition, he donated his house with its surrounding buildings."

"Is it only Russian art?" Blanche asked.

"Yes," Zhanna replied. "You will see portraits from the 18th century, realist paintings from the 19th century, and romantic canvases from the 20th century."

"Don't forget the icons," John reminded her. "Icon painters are usually anonymous, replicating an 'original' image. Some of you will recognize one of the icons, I'm sure. St. George and the Dragon. The Gallery has five of them, all with subtle differences."

As the group walked toward the entrance, John pointed to a stone image above the doorway. "That's also St. George slaying the dragon. It's more than fortuitous that he is the city's patron saint. The Gallery has been renovated since I was first here more than half a century ago, but St. George still looks down on the courtyard. He now sees, as you do, a protective iron fence and a towering statue of Anton Chekhov."

Once inside, Zhanna led the group to a ticket window. The cost of tickets was displayed in both Russian and English.

"I wish tickets were this cheap at the Metropolitan," Peter remarked.

"But they're still expensive," Francis chimed in. "And foreigners have to pay more than Russians. That's not fair."

"Do you have to pay like a foreigner?" Madge asked John. "After all, you own an apartment in Moscow."

"Even though I have an identity card from the Russian government, I'm still considered a foreigner. To be honest, Madge, I rarely pay like a foreigner when I go to exhibitions and the theater."

"Do you jump a turnstile?" Peter joked.

"The truth is that I rely on Russian friends. They buy a ticket for me while I wait off to one side of the line. Unlike many Muscovites, I never jump a turnstile."

With the group in tow, Zhanna moved to the exhibition halls. "Wander as you please in each hall, but don't stray out of sight. Stay with me, and I'll point out my favorite paintings."

In hall # 3 Zhanna paused in front of a woman's portrait from the 18th century. "Does anyone know who she is?"

"That's easy," Madge said, reading the English with her pince-nez glasses. "Catherine the Great, painted by Aleksei Antropov."

"Antropov is famous for his intense colors," Peter added. "As you can see from Catherine's cheeks, the pillow, and the chair, Antropov is addicted to various shades of red. It's a remarkable painting."

When the group got to hall # 8, Zhanna again paused in front of one of her favorites. "You've probably never heard of the painter, Orest Kiprensky, but I'll bet the name Aleksandr Pushkin rings a bell with all of you. Art critics say this portrait of the poet is the best ever done during his lifetime."

As they moved from portrait painters to realists, John felt in his element. He, too, had favorites.

"In view of your upcoming cruise," John said, "this painting may have special significance." He pointed to a work by Ilya Repin, *Volga Boatmen*. "This is not as famous as his *Barge Haulers on the Volga*, which is in St. Petersburg, but both paintings depict the grueling reality of life on the Volga for toiling laborers."

By way of contrast, John then moved to a winter scene in the countryside, *Zimoi*, by Konstantin Korobin. "It's idyllic. Look at the snow, the sled, the cottage—all nestled together as twilight descends."

"Deep down you're a romantic, not a realist," Zhanna said, brushing John's shoulder with an affectionate touch. "Let's show them two paintings by Vasilii Tropinin."

"They're lovely," Madge said, looking at *Kruzhevnitsa* and *Zolotoshveika* in exhibition hall # 13. "And they are so much alike."

"Indeed," Zhanna said. "It's the same young, attractive woman smiling at us as she makes lace with a golden needle in a silvery light. You can't help but fall in love with her."

"You will love the icons, too," John said as he and Zhanna led the group to another part of the Gallery.

"As I mentioned in the courtyard, the Gallery has five icons of St. George slaying the dragon. Legend has it that a dragon lived in a lake in Libya and that the local people, pagans, worshiped the dragon and appeased him by sacrificing their children to him. When the Queen's daughter was about to be sacrificed, St. George appeared on a white horse and slew the dragon."

"But the image in front of us shows St. George on a black horse, not a white one," Madge was quick to point out.

"That's what makes this image so unusual," John said. "Maybe that's why it's my favorite of the five in the Gallery. Icon artists replicate the same image with subtle differences and nuances."

"Over to our left," Zhanna said, "is Our Lady of Vladimir (*Bogomater' Vladimirovskaia*). It dates back to the 12th century. This icon of the Virgin pressing her Son to her cheek was carried by the Russian army in its battles against the Mongols, who burned Vladimir to the ground when it was the Russian capital. The 'icon writer' (*ikonopisets*) is unknown."

"What you will see next," John said, "is the most famous of all icons."

"Andrei Rublev's Holy Trinity," Peter said knowingly. "As a younger man I specialized in icons, you might say."

"The colors are gorgeous," Blanche said. "Look at the garments worn by those three angels, especially the one in the center. Bright blue cloak on one shoulder, rust brown garment on the other, and a gold colored sash. The ambiance is ethereal."

"Beautiful, but too expensive for us," Francis joked, shaking his head.

"Not really," John said. "Our next stop is the sales gallery, where you can buy poster reproductions for a song."

"With or without frames?" Francis asked.

"That's the rub," John admitted, remembering his own experience. "Not long ago I bought two posters for my home in the States. I had them framed locally. That set me back close to five hundred dollars."

"Let's skip the posters," Francis said. "I'm up for postcards."

On their way outside to the bus, John took Zhanna aside and said that he would meet her back at the ship in the evening. "I want to wander a bit."

"Would you mind if Madge and I joined you?" Peter asked. "I apologize for eaves-dropping."

"I'd love to have company. Over lunch you can tell me what you meant by your earlier comment that you once specialized in icons. Then we can head over to the river, where there's a bridge and a small park that are worth seeing. I go there often."

Five minutes later they were outside the Tretyakovsky metro station, on a narrow street with several eateries. Looking up at a McDonald's sign, Peter shook his head in disbelief. "You're not taking us there, are you?"

"No." John laughed. "I might have back in 1991 when the first McDonald's opened in Moscow. Russians stood in lines outside in a nearby park for hours just to get an American hamburger. When it was no longer a novelty with long queues, I confess that I did treat a Russian friend and his daughter to a Big Mac with fries."

"And today?" Madge asked.

"A McDonald's can be found in many parts of the city. Russians have become addicted to burgers and fries, but long lines have disappeared. A Russian competitor, *Bistro*, eventually emerged. But the chain hasn't become a successful rival in spite of government wishes."

"Are we going to a *Bistro*?" Madge asked.

"No. We're going to a place called *Matrëshka*. See that sign over there?" John asked, pointing to a red bow that framed three nesting dolls—a mother holding a samovar flanked by two little girls.

Once inside, they saw a sumptuous buffet in the center of room. "It's good," John said, "but I'm going to order my usual for all of us."

"And what might that be?" Madge asked. "Something very Russian, I'm sure."

"You'll soon see."

While they were sipping wine and nibbling at bread still warm from the oven, the waitress arrived with three round ceramic bowls. "Careful, hot," she said in limited English learned on the job.

"The crust on top makes me think it might be chicken pot pie," Madge said.

"That's not Russian," John said. "Take a peak under the crust."

"The red color is a giveaway." Peter smiled. "Borscht."

After a more than satisfying meal, topped off with a pot of aromatic tea, John turned to Peter. "Before we move on, would you like to tell me how you got interested in icons?"

"One might say that I was adventurous as a young entrepreneur." Peter paused, thinking back to the collapse of the Soviet Union. "When Lithuania became independent in 1991 there was money to be made by businessmen with the right connections. My Lithuanian heritage gave me what was needed."

"You became an exporter, importer," John guessed.

"I engaged in what is called the gray economy. I bought and sold icons."

"By 'gray' he means not entirely legal," Madge explained.

"It all started when President Yeltsin mandated shock therapy for the Russian economy," Peter said. "One result was galloping inflation, which wiped out personal savings overnight. The Finance Minister predicted that the rate of inflation in 1993 would be one thousand percent. In order to survive, Russians began selling their personal possessions."

"I saw that with my own eyes," John said. "The streets of Moscow were overflowing with people hawking their wares. Congestion near the Kremlin on streets like Tverskaia and Stoleshnikov was monumental."

"That's when I started to buy icons," Peter said.

"You did business in Russia?" John asked.

"I wasn't that foolish." Peter laughed. "Russians would travel to Lithuania with their contraband goods. It wasn't hard to find what I was looking for."

"Tell John how you got the icons out of Lithuania," Madge prompted.

"It was really quite simple. I have an acquaintance who works in the antiquarian department of the Lithuanian Ministry of Culture. For a modest fee, he did the paper work that permitted me to take my treasures out of the country. I had no trouble selling them when I got home."

"Now Peter is a paragon of virtue," Madge teased.

"On that note," John said, "let's join the newlyweds."

"A wedding?" Peter asked facetiously.

"You'll see."

Peter led them back to the Tretyakovsky Gallery and down Lavrushinsky Street to a footbridge crossing the Vodootvodny canal. "It's called the Bridge of Padlocks," John explained.

"What's that supposed to mean?" Madge asked. "It looks like a bridge with small Christmas trees."

Once on the bridge, Madge could see that the trees were made of iron and were decorated with an enormous number of padlocks. "Russians refer to them as Trees of Love," John said. "Newlyweds come to the bridge with padlocks to seal their love. Do you know what they do with the keys?"

"Keep them as mementos, I suppose," Peter guessed, incorrectly.

"They throw them into the water." John laughed.

"What's so funny?" Madge asked.

"The last time I was on the bridge I overheard a Russian giving advice to a newlywed couple. He said not to throw both keys into the water because the couple might want to unlock the padlock in the event of a divorce."

Standing in the middle of the bridge, John pointed to a towering statue far off in the distance. "That's Peter the Great at the helm of his ship. It's a monstrosity that St. Petersburg rejected. The Mayor of Moscow, however, fell in love with it. That's why it's here on the Moscow River, right next to Red October, a chocolate factory that makes my mouth water when I think of its savories."

At the end of the bridge they walked down to an island, where they were greeted by a memorial to the painter Ilya Repin. "This part of the island is known as Marshy Square (*Bolotnaia ploshchad*)," John said. "At the far end of the Square is a fantastic sculptural composition by Mikhail Shemiakin."

"I know him," Peter said. "He's a renowned Russian artist who lives in New York City. I met him once at an exhibition."

"Before coming to the States in 1981," John remarked, "he lived and worked in France for a decade. His works of art are in museums around the world. The sculptural composition in front of us was a gift by Shemiakin to the city of Moscow. It's called *Children are the Victims of Adults' Vices*."

"I see a boy and a girl with blindfolds," Madge said, focusing on two gold-colored bronze statues, on a platform, in front of thirteen gray bronze statues representing vices.

"The vices range from drug addiction and prostitution on the far left to poverty and war on the far right," John said. "Shemiakin wanted to draw attention to crimes against children so as to save mankind."

"That's a tall order," Peter said succinctly.

"Not to change the subject," John said, "but if you're interested in sculptures of a different sort we could make a couple of metro stops on our way back to the ship."

"Sounds good to me," Madge said. "Follow the leader."

Retracing their steps, they walked past the Tretyakovsky Gallery and over to the green line. "We get off at the first stop and then take an underground walkway, a *perekhod*, to a sister station, *Ploshchad' revoliutsii*. In English, Revolution Square. As you'll see, it has dozens of bronze sculptures in little alcoves. Soldiers, athletes, workers, farmers, and even school children."

"Do you have any favorites?" Madge asked when they arrived at their destination, adjacent to the Kremlin.

"Yes, but let's wander a bit so you get a feel for the revolutionary ambience."

Peter stopped in front of a bronze soldier, one hand on a rifle, the other on a dog. "That's interesting," he said. "Look at the dog's nose. It's almost golden."

"That's because school children rub it for good luck," John said. "Just like the muzzle of that soldier's revolver over there, resting on his knee."

"I can see that they're your favorites," Peter remarked.

"Yes, but there are seventy-two to chose from."

John let Peter and Madge admire them all before returning to the underground passageway that connects the blue line to the green line. "The green line will take us back to the ship, but we'll stop for a minute at the *Mayakovsky* station."

"Named for the bard of the revolution whose bust we saw at the cemetery," Madge said.

"Correct. It's one of the oldest stations on the metro system. It was built in 1938, thirty-three meters below ground. During the Second World War it was used as an air raid shelter."

Five minutes later Madge and Peter were admiring the jewel of the Moscow metro system. "Look at those white and pink marble walls," Madge said.

"And the mosaics on the ceiling," Peter added. "Wow."

"In all, there are thirty-four," John said. "All designed by a famous artist based on a Mayakovsky poem, *Moscow Sky*. Mayakovsky, a self-described communist futurist (*komfut*), was looking up to a bright Soviet future. Disillusioned, he took his own life."

"The mosaics are like Soviet posters," Peter remarked.

John concurred. "Everything from planes flying over the Kremlin to a peasant woman laboring in a wheat field. Works of art, nonetheless."

"I know that you've had enough for one day," John continued. "Don't worry. Our next stop will be our last stop, *Rechnoi vokzal*. From there, again, it's only a short walk to the ship. I'm going to skip dinner, but I'll see you in the morning when we begin our cruise on the Volga."

CHAPTER 4

After a quick breakfast in his apartment, John tidied the place up in preparation for a ten-day absence from Moscow. When he emerged from the building with a small suitcase on rollers, he walked up to the market place and boarded a bus that took him to a park just across the street from an alabaster statue of a woman holding a ship above her head. She welcomes one and all to Moscow's Northern River Port.

The main building is a massive granite structure with a tower that still sports, in relief, an almost invisible Soviet hammer and sickle. One can easily miss this relic from the communist past. Striking, however, are twelve mosaics embedded vertically in four pillars. Each depicts, at the center of a white circle, a maritime scene. After pausing to admire his favorites, John walked around the building to the docking area. Three ships, including the *Novikov Priboi*, were moored side by side at a quay advertising cold beer, ice cream, pizza, and a meat dish called *shaurma*. The *Novikov Priboi* was preparing for departure. The ship's name, in gold letters on its side, was being polished by a deck hand who leaned precariously over the railing, mop in hand. Another member of the crew was winching a thick blue rope at the stern of the ship. Soon martial music would be played over a loudspeaker, signifying that the *Novikov Priboi* was on its way to the main channel of the Moscow-Volga canal.

After a brief visit to his cabin, John joined everyone on deck. The ship began to move in slow motion. Martial music inspired some passengers to clap and do a jig. "You have to love it," Blanche said to Zhanna.

"If you like marches from the Soviet era," Neville said, shaking his head in disapproval.

"Don't be so negative," Moody said with some reluctance. She rarely criticized her husband. "Think of John Philip Souza."

"What's over there on the opposite shore?" Madge asked. "It looks like a submarine."

"It's a tourist attraction, along with the seaplane next to it," Zhanna answered. "It's part of the Northern Tushino Park for Culture and Rest."

When the port facilities, gantries and all, were out of sight, John provided background information to those within earshot. "Before we reach the Volga, we will have traveled about eighty miles through eleven locks. The Moscow-Volga canal was one of Stalin's major construction projects of the thirties."

"At an enormous cost," Zhanna added.

"How much?" Francis asked.

"I was thinking of human life, not money," Zhanna replied sadly. "Forced labor was at its peak. Thousands, maybe millions, perished on construction projects. The economic goal, not human life, was the end-all for Stalin."

"In 1947, marking the 10th anniversary of the Moscow-Volga Canal, the government issued a memorial stamp," John added. "The color is symbolic, at least for me. Bloodred."

"Russians must have short memories," Neville commented. "Journalists write that Stalin is no longer reviled."

"It's complicated," John explained. "Surveys show that during times of crisis Russians exhibit nostalgia for the Soviet past and for leaders like Lenin and Stalin. The misery index that climbed precipitously during the Yeltsin years has abated, but life for pensioners and life in the countryside remains precarious. In a recent poll more respondents felt that there was progress under Stalin than those who felt that Stalin caused colossal harm to the nation."

"Communist demonstrations here in Moscow are no longer the drawing card that they were some years ago," Zhanna added, "but nostalgia for the past is particularly high in cities like Voronezh."

"Voronezh was a major hub in the Soviet military complex," John explained. "There was a furor not long ago when ten huge billboards suddenly appeared on the streets of Voronezh in honor of Stalin's 130th birthday. He was pictured in military uniform against a bright red background. There was a Soviet flag, of course, along with the slogan *Victory will Follow.*"

"If you want my professional opinion," Francis offered, "Stalin was a classic narcissist, not someone to be admired. He was self-centered, oversensitive to criticism, and unable to feel sympathy for others. A professor of psychiatry at Cornell University takes the diagnosis one step further. Otto Kernberg, an expert on personality disorders, sees Stalin as a malignant narcissist."

"What's the difference?" Neville asked.

"In addition to exhibiting the classic traits of narcissism, a malignant narcissist is paranoid, aggressive, and antisocial. Moral and ethical behavior fall by the wayside." Francis fell silent, thinking back to his own behavior not too long ago when he testified in a bitter divorce case involving child custody.

"What do Russian leaders think of Stalin?" Peter asked.

"Recently," John answered, "Prime Minister Putin spoke about Stalin at a site in the southern part of Moscow where mass executions took place in the 1930s. He repeatedly used the word 'tragedy' to describe what he called the colossal cruelty of Stalin. Putin urged those attending the ceremony at Butovo to remember the past and to make sure that it is never forgotten."

"Why, then, does Putin get such a bad press in the West?" Blanche asked.

"His KGB past," Neville answered.

"Well, that's only part of it," John said. "Like 79% of Russian respondents in a national poll, Putin regrets the demise of the Soviet Union. In an interview with the newspaper *Komsomol'skaia Pravda* he stated that those who do not regret the end of the Union have no heart."

"There you have it," Neville said. "Putin wants to return to the Soviet past."

"That's not what Putin meant in the interview," John replied. "He also stated that those who want to revive the Union in its previous form have no head."

"What about President Medvedev?" Peter asked.

"You should read the lengthy interview that he gave in May 2010 on the eve of Victory Day," Zhanna interjected.

"What's Victory Day?" Moody asked.

"That's the day when we defeated Germany. It's still an emotional day for all Russians. We lost millions of lives. Stalin put the figure at fourteen million. Khrushchev and Brezhnev referred to twenty million. Gorbachev went even higher, twenty-seven million. In an interview with *Izvestiia*, President Medvedev praised Stalin for some 'strong decisions' during the Great Patriotic War."

"But we shouldn't take that remark out of context," John said. "The interview in its entirety is a blistering attack on Stalin. Medvedev said quite bluntly that Stalin could never be forgiven for the crimes he committed against his own people. But Medvedev opposed painting all Soviet history black. There were also bright pages, he stated. As for the renaissance of Stalinism, Medvedev emphasized that individuals have the right to love or to hate Stalin. However, Stalinism in the daily life of Russians will not be tolerated. Medvedev warned that billboards glorifying Stalin, like the ones in Voronezh, are beyond the pale."

When the novelty of Stalin's massive locks wore off, passengers put away their cameras. Some continued to stand by the railing, chatting, while others seated themselves around small white tables on the bright blue deck. They were content just to bask in the autumn sunshine. The morning chill was completely gone by the time luncheon was served. After wining and dining, passengers either returned topside or went to their cabins to freshen up. There was nothing scheduled until late afternoon when the ship's captain would host a pre-dinner reception with caviar and Russian pancakes. Those on deck would first be treated to a sunset that turned the surface of the water into a shimmering red blanket.

When dawn came the next day the *Novikov Priboi* was on its way in slow motion to the shores of Uglich, a tenth-century town on the Volga. Legend has it that the town's first coat of arms had a gigantic raven that supposedly flew at night over the town to ward off danger. If the raven sensed danger it would cry out with a loud caw, caw, and would flap its large wings. Unfortunately, the raven failed in its mission. Uglich was burned to the ground many times, all the way back to the 13th century when Tatars were the dominant force. But when the *Novikov Priboi* approached Uglich it could not have been more peaceful. It was a dream. Three gorgeous churches with sparkling domes rose above a small forest of trees on the coastline.

"See that church with the red turret and blue onion domes?" Zhanna asked the small group around her. "It's called the Church of Dimitry. Does anyone know who Dimitry was?"

When no one replied, John raised his hand. "He was the son of Ivan the Terrible and his seventh wife."

"Seven wives?" Peter laughed, remembering the bridge of locks in Moscow. "He must have kept a pocketful of keys."

"Dimitry died of a stab wound," Zhanna continued.

"Murder?" Neville asked.

"It might have been an accident during an epileptic seizure, but the popular belief was that Dimitry's death was murder."

"Residents were alerted to his death by peels from the bell tower of the *Spaso-Preobrazhenskii* cathedral," John added. "The population flocked to the cathedral, killing suspects en masse. Not even the bell was spared."

"The bell?" Neville asked.

"All that I know," John answered, "is that the bell was shipped off to Siberia. It was returned to Uglich three hundred years later."

"When we get our feet on terra firma," Zhanna said, "our first stop will be the Church of Dimitry-on-the-Blood, as it is officially called. It was built on the site of Dimitry's death."

On their way to the church, John pointed to a flag with Uglich's coat of arms. "The black raven has long since disappeared," he said. "What you see now is an image of the young Dimitry. That's a golden halo around his head and a silver knife in his right hand."

"The dominant color is crimson," Moody noted. "Is it supposed to represent blood?"

"Probably not," Zhanna said. "For me the colors taken together symbolize *derzhava*, power."

Once inside the church, the group couldn't take its eyes off the frescoes.

"It's as if we're back in the Tretyakovsky Gallery," Moody said. "We're surrounded by beautiful pastels, including one that I recognize. The Holy Trinity."

After the ubiquitous treasures had been carefully examined and fully appreciated, the group sat down on benches for their next treat. Four young men appeared and stood in front of a panorama of frescoes. Dressed in black frocks, they looked down at the books that they held. A hush came over the room as they began to sing in stentorian voices.

"That was wonderful," Blanche said when the concert of choral music ended.

"If you want to purchase a tape," John said to the group, "copies are on sale at the door."

"Everyone wants to make money," Francis commented.

"Russians call it wild capitalism," John said. "Soon you'll become acquainted with another aspect of Russian life."

After leaving the church, Zhanna guided the group to the Museum of Russian Vodka. "Uglich was home for the Vodka King, Smirnov, in the 19th century," she explained. "Russians celebrate their most beloved alcoholic drink on January 31st."

"Does that mean that we have to wait five months for a glass of vodka?" Peter asked with a straight face.

"That might have been true under Gorbachev," John replied. "You may have read that he tried to control alcoholism by banning the sale of vodka."

"Tell them what you did," Zhanna urged.

"I would go to a farmers' market, the *Leningradskii rynok*, and look for vendors 'from the south,' as they are called. I could always find a Georgian who had a bottle of vodka for sale from under his table. He first made sure that there were no police in sight."

"How about you, Zhanna?" Madge asked.

"Like John I had my vodka, but I used it as currency."

"Let me explain." John chuckled. "During the Gorbachev years you could buy a favor or two for a bottle of vodka. Then, when the Soviet Union collapsed, Yeltsin promulgated economic reforms that were catastrophic for the population. In practical terms, the ruble was worthless for a number of years. Vodka, on the other hand, was almost as good as gold."

"All this talk about vodka is making me thirsty," Neville joked.

"Be patient," John replied with a smile. "Only one more stop before heading back to the ship."

"First you're going to meet Baba Yaga," Zhanna said with a twinkle in her eye.

"Who's that?" Neville asked. "A Russian diplomat?"

"Ask any Russian child," John replied. "Baba Yaga is a folklore witch who lives in the forest, in a hut built on chicken legs which is surrounded by a fence of bones to keep intruders out. When she appears, a wild wind begins to blow, trees shake, and leaves whirl through the air."

"Sounds terrifying," Moody said.

"Yes, but Russian children know that Baba Yaga can be kind and helpful to the pure of heart, to those who seek wisdom, knowledge, and truth," Zhanna explained.

"If I may," John said, "I want to tell you folks a real life story. During the Great Patriotic War, many Russian children were evacuated to Uglich for safety. My best friend was a youngster whose parents sent him here to live with an aunt. One day, while on a walk in the forest, he saw what he thought was a witch with a long pointed nose. She was standing behind a fence in front of a small wooden cottage. Baba Yaga? My friend was terrified, but he nonetheless accepted her invitation to enter the cottage. Baba Yaga turned out to be a kind old lady, in spite of her looks, and my friend looked forward to seeing her again."

"Did he go there often?" Moody asked.

"Unfortunately, my friend's story has a sad ending. Like the witch Baba Yaga, the old lady slept on top of an ancient brick oven. One night she was burned to death when her cottage caught fire. Needless to say, my friend still remembers in great detail his Baba Yaga."

"In front of us is the Museum of Myths and Superstition," Zhanna said. "We thought you might like to see it even though it's really a place for children. It's part of Russian culture."

"The youngsters ahead of us," John said as he led the way into a two-story wooden building, "are no doubt from a local kindergarten, a *detskii sad*."

"Why are they taking their shoes off?" Blanche asked.

"Well," Zhanna answered with smile, "the children will see not only Baba Yaga and witches but also goblins. All dolls, of course. The children know from fairy tales that they must put their left shoe on their right foot and their right shoe on their left foot in order to be accepted by goblins as one of their own."

"I'll pass on that," Francis said. "It might jeopardize my standing as a child psychologist."

Everyone laughed, including the bearded museum owner and his well-known artist wife. The *Novikov Priboi* group got a cook's tour of the museum. They all declined, however, a witch's brew that was offered by a goblin at the end of the tour.

"I'm ready for a real drink," Neville said.

"It won't be long now," John replied. "We're headed back to the ship. The chef, not a goblin, is preparing a shashlik meal for us."

Food was followed by music in the lounge. Stepping up to the bar, Neville ordered his third vodka. Zhanna was standing next to him.

"What are you drinking?" Neville asked.

"*Yablochnii sok*, apple juice."

"How about something stronger?" he asked, brushing her forearm with his hand.

"No thanks. I'm fine."

"You add excitement to the cruise," Neville said. "I love listening to you. Your English is flawless."

"If I didn't know better, I'd say that you're flirting with me," Zhanna said with a wink.

"Caught me," Neville confessed, hands up in the air. "Nothing ventured, nothing gained."

As Neville moved away, John joined Zhanna. "Want to hear something amusing?" she asked.

"Let me guess," John replied. "I was watching our diplomat in action. He has a roving eye. At least he has good taste."

Zhanna blushed. "Now you're flirting, John."

"I'm too old for you."

The applause that followed was not for John. It was for the accordion player, who bowed after his last number and announced that the ship would be sailing in the morning to Kostroma, famous for its wooden architecture, and then on to Yaroslavl, the oldest city on the Volga and a UNESCO World Heritage Site.

CHAPTER 5

After a buffet breakfast, Zhanna left the *Novikov Priboi* and raised a little flag for all to see. Surrounded by familiar faces, she then headed off toward the National Museum of Wooden Architecture, located on the western side of the city where the Kostroma and Volga rivers meet. Along the way they stopped in front of a towering statue on a concrete pedestal.

"Isn't that Lenin?" Neville asked.

"Yes," Zhanna replied. "Some cities still keep Lenin center stage."

"Like the Siberian city of Ulan-Ude," John added. "The statue there is gigantic."

"We saw Lenin in the mausoleum," Francis said, "but that was it."

"The city of Moscow passed legislation," John explained, "permitting only a few statues of Lenin to remain on public display."

"What about Stalin?" Blanche asked.

"There are two that come to mind," John said. "There's the one by his grave next to the Kremlin Wall, and there's another not far from Gorky Park. It's in a small, fenced off area that has become the final resting place for statues of Soviet leaders in disrepute."

"Ahead of us," Zhanna said as they approached a bridge at the confluence of the Kostroma and Volga rivers, "is the Ipatevsky monastery. The territory is divided into two parts, the old town and the new town. The new town is not so new. It was built in the 17th century and is home for the Museum of Wooden Architecture. That's a misnomer, by the way."

"How come?" Blanche asked.

"The museum is actually a reserve, an outdoor museum, a *zapovednik*," Zhanna replied. "Wooden churches, cottages, and bathhouses have been assembled from surrounding villages. As you'll see, they're nestled together amongst birch trees and streams."

"The windows in the houses are so small," Madge commented when they got to the reserve. "I suppose there's an explanation."

"Small windows minimized heat loss during the winter months."

"Is there special significance to the wooden carvings above the windows?" Peter asked.

"Not that I know of," Zhanna replied. "Like the flowers you see, they add a touch of rustic beauty to the cottages."

At the end of the outdoor museum tour, three women in colorful folk attire emerged from nowhere. They began to dance to music from an accordion. The circle of three soon became a circle of five when Blanche and Madge joined hands with the Russian ensemble. Everyone was smiling as the group left the reserve, heading back to the *Novikov Priboi* for lunch to be followed by an open discussion with John while the ship wound its way north to Yaroslavl.

"Today's discussion," John began as passengers settled back in not-so-comfortable chairs, "concerns corruption and bribery in Russia. We touched on this topic briefly when we talked about the road police. I'm going to kick off what I hope will be a give-and-take discussion with a statistic. Some of you may have heard of Transparency International. It's an organization that monitors the level of corruption in countries around the world. Last year Russia ranked near the bottom, 154th out of a total of one hundred and seventy-eight nations. President Medvedev has called corruption enemy number one for a free and just society. He points to corruption as the main problem for the Russian economy. Twenty-nine percent of Russian respondents in a national poll acknowledged that they or a member of their family had paid a bribe during the previous twelve months. The figure rose to forty-two percent of respondents in Moscow, the hub of corruption and home for entrenched bureaucrats, *chinovniki*."

A question came from the back of the room. "Isn't that why the Mayor of Moscow was recently removed from office?"

"That's an interesting story," John replied. "Let me start with Mayor Luzhkov's predecessor, Gavril Popov. In 1991 Popov said that if a bureaucrat took 15-20% for signing a contract or document, he was an honest *chinovnik*. Anything higher was bribery. Seven months later,

President Yeltsin chose Luzhkov to run the city of Moscow. During Luzhkov's long tenure in office, the Popov percentage grew many times over. Corruption figured prominently in Luzhkov's removal last spring by President Medvedev, although officially it was due to what Medvedev called a loss of confidence (*doverie*) in Luzhkov."

"I've heard that everyone is on the take," Neville commented when John paused in his story.

"Potentially, yes," John said. "In first place in what one Russian newspaper called the hit parade of bribe takers are the police, customs officials, and law enforcement agencies. The silver medal goes to the traffic police. Third place goes to members of the judicial system."

Francis turned to Neville and whispered a comment about the American judiciary. "Our judges may not take bribes, like in Russia, but they are not always fair. I once testified as an expert witness in a child custody case. When I diagnosed the father as meeting the criteria for Narcissistic Personality Disorder (NPD), the father charged in a letter to the American Psychological Association's Office that I was incompetent and unethical. I complained to the presiding judge, who obviously didn't like the father. But it was not a matter of law. If it had been, the judge clearly would have exercised his discretionary power to help me. He has been admonished at least once by a state commission for misconduct."

A gentleman in the front row raised his hand. He had a comment and a question for John. "Not too long ago Nancy Pelosi sponsored a resolution condemning what she called a culture of corruption on the other side of the aisle. Over here the culture seems to be everywhere. Who profits the most from Russian bribes?"

"Bribes are fairly small," John said. "Almost two-thirds range between 500 and 10,000 rubles (roughly twenty to four hundred dollars). Only 2.7% of all bribes are really lucrative."

"Who gets the big ones?" Francis asked.

"A psychiatrist once got $10,000 for a draft exemption," John replied, smiling at the psychologist in front of him, "but it's top bureaucrats who take the cake. A senior Russian prosecutor estimates that corrupt officials pocket about one hundred and twenty billion dollars annually. That includes low level bureaucrats as well as senior *chinovniki*. At the top, one name comes to mind. Mikhail Kasyanov, a former Minister of Finance, was nicknamed 'Misha 2%' for money allegedly received from suppliants. Not all bureaucrats can be bribed, however. The general in charge of fighting organized crime turned down an offer of $5,000 a month, although he openly acknowledged in a popular weekly newspaper that the level of corruption among his colleagues was very high."

"If bribery is so pervasive, why is it that the Russian billionaire Khodorkovsky is sitting in a Siberian penal colony?" Neville asked.

"He had the wrong mind-set," John answered. "He once told a friend that with money you can ultimately buy anything. Unlike other Russians who made fortunes in the Yeltsin era through shady deals, Khodorkovsky chose not to seek asylum abroad. He remained in Russia and was convicted of fraud, tax evasion, and money laundering."

"It sounds hopeless to me," Neville said, shaking his head. "Do Russian leaders really care about corruption and bribery in their country? As you've noted, John, the worst offenders are bureaucrats. With good reason the political party supporting Putin and Medvedev is called the party of bureaucrats."

"If the Procurator General was correct when he stated that eighty percent of Russian bureaucrats have been compromised with bribes, then the picture is indeed bleak," John responded. "But some promising steps have been taken. It is now mandatory for *chinovniki* to declare their income, their expenses, and their real estate holdings. If actually implemented, that legislation should help. In an address to law enforcement *chinovniki* Putin said that power and money must be separated. If you want to make money, he said, go into business. If you want to serve the state, live on a government salary."

"That'll be the day," a skeptic in the front row mumbled.

"Looking specifically at the police," John continued, "there has been real reform."

"Sure," the skeptic said out loud. "There's been a name change. The men in uniform are now called policemen, not militiamen. Big deal."

"It's not just a name change," John explained. "Re-accreditation is underway. The police force is being trimmed by about twenty percent. New hires will have to have a legal education, while officers already on duty will have to take special courses. In the past the police were feared almost as much as criminals, but now there is hope. Polls indicate a significant drop in the number of Russians who distrust the police. Confidence in the police has risen noticeably among 'status citizens,' among those who are better educated and better off financially."

"Probably no one here, except for John and me," Zhanna said, "paid any attention to the billboard being put up on the pathway to our ship. In bold print it refers to bribes and to a specific article of the Russian Criminal Code. In short, it is now a crime to give a bribe, to take a bribe, or to be a middleman in any such transaction."

"What's the punishment?" Francis asked.

"According to the legislative bill," John said, "if the bribe is less than the ruble equivalent of a thousand dollars, there will be a fine of fifty times the amount of the bribe. At the high end of the scale, if the bribe exceeds the equivalent of forty thousand dollars the fine will be one hundred times the amount of the bribe but not to exceed twenty million dollars."

"No prison time?" Francis asked.

"Oh, yes," John replied. "In the most egregious cases, the bill introduced by Medvedev provides for jail sentences as well as for the confiscation of property."

"Will judges go along with the new rules?" Peter asked.

"We'll see," John said. "Seeking to maximize their independence, Medvedev has proposed that no one be appointed to the bench if there are lawyers or notary publics in that person's family."

"Medvedev sounds serious about fighting corruption," Neville said, "but what about Putin?"

"That's a concern," John acknowledged. "Even before Putin decided to return to the presidency, a national survey indicated that 48% of the population doubted Medvedev's fight against corruption would be effective. Now there is even more concern. Putin's tenacious hold on political power has led to unflattering comparisons with Brezhnev by Russian commentators."

"A spokesperson for Putin recently caused liberal-minded Russians to shudder," Zhanna interjected. "The spokesperson told an internet station that Brezhnev was a huge plus, not a minus, for the history of our country. Let's hope that Gogol's satire on Russian corruption and officialdom remains one of Putin's favorite books. At least in words, if not deeds, Putin wants to combat corruption in Russia."

"One final comment," John said. "The President of the National Anti-Corruption Committee argued that in addition to fines and judicial reform, two things are needed for an effective campaign against corruption. First, political competition. Second, popular impatience with corruption. That's a tall order. Putin's party is becoming more dominant with every election, and polling data show that younger Russians are more tolerant of corruption than their parents. One needs to have faith in a refrain from a popular Russian song: *Tomorrow will be Better.*"

"It's probably time to leave crime and punishment behind," Zhanna suggested, with a nod to John. "The bar is open."

"Isn't it always open?" Neville asked hopefully. "Anyone care to join me?"

"I'm ready for a drink," Francis told Neville in a low voice as they moved into the corridor. "The other day you mentioned in passing that you focus on morality and ethics in one of the courses that you teach. I have a couple of questions."

"So do I," Neville said. "About the child custody case that you mentioned."

"Let's sit over there in the corner," Francis said. "We'll have some privacy."

"Stolichnaya for me," Neville said, winking at the buxom blond who was serving drinks. "Make it a double."

"Fifty grams?"

"Sounds good to me."

"I'd like a draft beer," Francis said.

With drinks in hand, Francis and Neville settled into soft leather chairs at a table for two.

"Okay," Neville said. "Tell me more about the child custody case. What was the outcome?"

"Although the judge disliked the father, he ruled against the mother in favor of joint custody for the two young girls."

"What happened?" Neville asked.

"Well, it was partially my fault," Francis admitted. "I stated in my report to the court and in oral testimony that the father met the criteria for Narcissistic Personality Disorder. I argued that he showed a lack of empathy for the feelings of others, that he was self-centered, and that he had an exaggerated sense of importance and entitlement.

I told the court that my conclusions were based on a reading of data from the Minnesota Multiphasic Personality Inventory test."

"Sounds convincing to me," Neville said. "Did the judge challenge the data?"

"It wasn't the judge," Francis said. "I purposely withheld from the court the raw data and the computerized report. After repeated requests from the father, I eventually sent him the raw data. But I didn't send the three-page computerized report about the findings, figuring that a layman like the father would not be able to interpret the data on his own. An examination of validity tests and clinical scales can be daunting, even for a trained psychologist."

"Withholding information was probably unethical," Neville sighed. "Especially if the data did not support your conclusion."

"To make a long story short, the father analyzed the raw data and gave his attorney a six-page report challenging my diagnosis. The attorney made it clear to the court that at the very least I had misinterpreted the raw data. I may be many things, but I am not incompetent."

"In other words, you knew that you were giving false testimony to the court. Why would you do that?"

"Before I answer, I need some vodka." Francis went to the bar and came back with not one but two glasses of what Russians call the green snake.

"The mother bribed me."

"What?" Neville asked, astonished but not naïve, having himself crossed the line between morality and immorality more than once.

"I had just gone through a bitter divorce. My ex-wife took me to the cleaners, and my private practice was languishing. I was forced to file for bankruptcy. When I was offered $5,000 to write a family evaluation that would help a mother win custody of her two young daughters, I couldn't resist. I needed the money, and I truly believe, as I stated in my recommendations to the court, that teenage girls need a mom on a daily basis to reinforce the idea that women can be intelligent and feminine."

"Wow," Neville said in a low voice. "You didn't feel bad when it was all over?"

"Not really. My recommendations did not hurt the father because the judge rejected them. The mother's cause was lost only because a court-appointed law guardian stated that the youngest daughter had said in an interview with her that she would run away from home if forced to live with her mother. In practice, both girls ended up living with their father. The court nonetheless ordered the father to pay child support to the mother. In other words, the mother didn't really lose the five thousand dollars that she gave me for writing a misleading family evaluation."

"That's one way of looking at it," Neville said.

"Who's looking? At what?" Moody asked when she and Blanche materialized within earshot. "We just wanted to let you know that Yaroslavl is on the horizon. Let's go up on deck for a look-see. It's getting dark. In the morning we'll have a tour of what our travel brochure calls the oldest and largest of the eight fortified cities in the Golden Ring around Moscow."

CHAPTER 6

When passengers disembarked in the morning for their tour of Yaroslavl, they were not impressed by their immediate surroundings. A lackluster port belies the beauty of Yaroslavl and conveys nothing about the city's rich history. When the group returned to the *Novikov Priboi* for lunch, however, they understood why tourists give kudos to Yaroslavl.

Most of the morning was spent at the *Spaso-Preobrazhenskii* monastery with its thick white walls, watchtowers, and embattlements.

"It's a veritable fortress," someone remarked.

"One of many in the Golden Ring," Zhanna reminded her group. "It was impregnable. The walls protected people and churches from attack. In the 16th century the *muzhiks* from Yaroslavl, as Gogol called the peasant army, launched a counterattack against Polish invaders. The peasants moved south and liberated Moscow, decapitating prisoners in Red Square with their scythes and pulling out ribs of suspected traitors with hot irons."

"Ghastly!" Moody exclaimed.

"Today," John said, looking at Neville for a possible comment, "Yaroslavl hopes to promote security through different methods on a global level."

"I know what you're fishing for," Neville the retired diplomat said. "Yaroslavl's Third Annual Global Policy Forum just ended. One of the main issues was global security. All I can say is good luck."

"According to last week's press releases," Zhanna said, "there were over four hundred participants from thirty-six countries."

"Including an American Cold Warrior of Polish origin," John added with a chuckle. "I wonder what our former National Security Advisor thinks about the *muzhiks* from Yaroslavl."

As Zhanna guided her charges through the monastery complex, they stopped at cathedrals with green onion domes, looked up at a tower with gold maces, and admired a treasure-trove of icons. The entrance to one church was particularly impressive.

"Look at the curved archway," Madge said. "It reminds me of a rainbow." Once inside, the colors were even more spectacular. Flickering candles highlighted a panoply of frescoes painted in delicate hues of blue, red, and gold.

Zhanna interrupted the group's rapture. "It's time to head back to the ship. The captain's waiting. We'll soon be on our way to the Rybinsk Reservoir. Like the Moscow-Volga Canal, it's another one of Stalin's pet projects."

"Also at great cost," John added. "Some call it a massive flood basin. Others refer to it as a huge artificial lake, some five thousand square miles in size. One ancient town disappeared under water, and over a hundred thousand people had to be resettled. In the eyes of environmentalists, it was also an ecological disaster."

"The good old days," Neville said with sarcasm. "They'll never learn."

Crossing the Rybinsk Reservoir would take most of the afternoon. After lunch, with only water to look at, some passengers dozed off in deck chairs. Others went down to the ship's library. Zhanna and John chose the lounge. They could use the quiet time for conversation and a drink.

"It's nice to relax," John said, sipping a glass of Georgian red wine. "Getting to know the passengers?"

"That's a tall order," Zhanna responded. "We have so many guests on board. How about you?"

"As you know, I like working on these cruises as a study leader because I meet people with different backgrounds and experiences. It's early in the trip, but I find Peter and Madge the most interesting couple. On every cruise I meet a few people with whom I keep in touch after the cruise. I'm sure I'll see the Krukases again in the States. I'd like to see Peter's art gallery."

"Did I tell you that my father might join us when the ship gets to St. Petersburg?"

"No," John answered. "What's Viktor up to these days? It's been a while."

"An occasional engineering project, but nothing like the work he did before retirement. You probably know that he was one of the engineers who worked night and day under Brezhnev to construct the rail line from Taishet to Komsomolsk-on-Amur."

"Yes, the BAM railroad, which Brezhnev believed would provide access to raw materials north of the Trans-Siberian railroad and would be more secure from a possible Chinese attack."

"That's how my father met his first American friend, Michael Rayback."

"I know. He told me that they met on the Trans-Siberian, and that they became close friends in the years that followed."

"What actually happened," Zhanna explained, "is that when Rayback boarded the train in Moscow, he was pleasantly surprised to find that the second occupant in his compartment was an attractive young woman. She, however, got cold feet about spending four days and nights with an American who might get the wrong idea about travel on a Russian train. When she sought a replacement, Viktor was more than willing to swap compartments."

"Even though I never met Rayback," John said, "I know about his grave in the Novodevichy cemetery. I pointed it out to our group a few days ago. Neville Ogleby was surprised, to say the least. He said that Rayback had been department chair at his university. Francis Pickle seemed to have something on his mind, too, but he didn't say a word. He just stared at the concrete marker covered with fresh flowers."

While Zhanna and John sipped their second glass of wine, music filled the air. None of the guests recognized the female voice on the CD, but Zhanna smiled. "We have something in common, our first name."

As Zhanna Bichevskaia sang *Pod muzyku Vivaldi,* John stared off into space. He was lost in thought. "Vivaldi is one of my favorite composers. The mention of his name triggers memories."

"Care to share them with me?"

"Sure. No reason to keep secrets from you."

"You never talk about your wife. Is she one of the memories?"

"I suppose they start with her. We're divorced, you know."

"Was it amicable?"

"After twenty years of marriage, we just grew apart. Different goals, different aspirations, different interests. We stayed together until our daughter started college. Our daughter is now a journalist, traveling around the world to exotic places. Her mother prefers the comforts of life in the United States. We traveled together to Russia only once, when it was the Soviet Union. After that trip she told me that I should have married a Russian."

"But you never did," Zhanna remarked. "In fact, you're still single after how many years?"

"I can't remember," John joked. "What about you?"

"Divorced at age twenty-two. Seven months of marriage was enough for me. I'm sure Viktor told you about my husband. Drank too much. Didn't want me to have a career. Expected me to be submissive. Russian men are not the best husbands. I've dated since my divorce, but nothing serious. I prefer men as friends rather than spouses."

"We're on the same wavelength," John responded. "Friendship is what counts. I have to confess, though, that I had one serious relationship soon after my divorce."

"Tell me more. I'm all ears as you Americans say."

"As you know, I was a professor for many years. In addition to my regular course load, I also taught students in an independent degree study program that brought graduate students of all ages to campus for two weeks every summer. It was a great program with students from all walks of life. One of the students was a woman from New York City. To make a long story short, we liked each other. When she left campus after the first of two required summer sessions, she gave me her telephone number. Needless to say, I called. I got a secretary at the U.S. Commerce Department." John grinned, recalling his naiveté.

"Tell me the rest," Zhanna insisted.

"Well, we agreed to meet one Friday afternoon at a lounge in New York City's Grand Hyatt Hotel. We had drinks and listened to Vivaldi's Four Seasons."

"I assume she wasn't a secretary," Zhanna prompted with a smile.

"No." John laughed. "On my second visit she said that she had something to confess. The Commerce Department was a front for the Central Intelligence Agency. She and her husband, whom I never met, were both covert operatives. During another rendezvous at the Grand Hyatt she admitted that it had been necessary to get CIA permission to meet with me. I guess the Agency thought that my contacts in the Soviet Union might be helpful at some future date."

"You're not going to tell me that you signed up as a spy," Zhanna said with a disturbed look on her face.

"No, but I have to admit that right after graduating from college I was interested in the CIA's Junior Officer Training Program. In those days young educated people were attracted to the Agency."

"Not unlike our KGB," Zhanna commented. "After Brezhnev's death the security apparatus was modernized to attract young people. The KGB received the most favorable rating of twenty-three institutions in public opinion polls conducted in the 1990s."

"Looking back," John said, "I'm certainly glad that my application was rejected by the CIA."

"You weren't spooky enough?" Zhanna asked, grinning like a Halloween pumpkin.

"After a lengthy background check," John replied in all seriousness, "I was designated a security risk. During the McCarthy era any American with an interest in the Soviet Union was suspect in the eyes of Washington bureaucrats."

"Were you upset?"

"At first, yes. I didn't like my loyalty being questioned. You know what's ironic, though? I served in the military and was given a secret clearance. Later, during the Reagan years, I was given a certificate of appreciation for helping to win the Cold War."

"I have a certificate from the *Komsomol*, the Communist Youth Organization," Zhanna said with a straight face. "For services rendered."

"What's that supposed to mean?"

"Like most university students I joined the *Komsomol*, which, as you know, was a mass organization with millions of members. In addition to studying, I worked in a library. My job was to make sure that there was no subversive literature on the shelves. One day I removed a book by Solzhenitsyn. I received a certificate of commendation from the powers that be for my diligence." Zhanna started to laugh.

"What's so funny?"

"To be honest, which I wasn't with my superiors, I found two copies of the book. I removed only one."

"You're a sly one, Zhanna. My friend in New York would be impressed."

"Do you still keep in touch with her?"

"Yes, but not like in the old days. Early in our relationship she thought about leaving her husband, but he threw down the gauntlet. If she left, he would make sure that she never saw their son again. Faced with that threat, she stayed with her husband. We didn't stop seeing each other, but it was sporadic. Nowadays we're intimate friends, not passionate lovers."

"Has she ever visited you in Moscow?"

"No. That's hard to believe, I know. A few years ago she was my proxy at a dinner in New York, giving my classmates an update on my travels. They asked questions and were surprised, to say the least, that she had never visited me in Moscow. When I'm back in the States we have an occasional weekend together. On the qt of course."

"What does that mean?"

"It means that she doesn't tell her husband. I'm supposedly thousands of miles away."

"Now that you are retired, living for the most part here in Moscow, what do you do when you're not a study leader? You have a lot of free time on your hands."

"In addition to swimming at a pool three metro stops away, I visit friends, take in exhibitions, go to the theater, and shop. Every now and then I help a Russian friend who administers an exchange program between Russian and American universities. It gives me a chance to visit far-off places in Siberia and the Far East. I also have plenty of time to read and write. I'm partial to mystery novels."

"And writing?"

"I've given up on academic treatises that almost no one reads. Right now I'm working on a manuscript about the changes that I have seen and experienced in the Soviet Union and Russia since the death of Stalin."

"What do you find most striking?"

"Russia is now a much more open society. I'll give you an example that is close to my heart and my wallet. During the Khrushchev and Brezhnev eras, tourists had to stay at hotels. You know all about that, Zhanna. You worked for Intourist. It was also against Soviet law, which I didn't always obey, to sleep overnight in a Russian friend's apartment. Things changed under Gorbachev. I was able to live a whole year in an apartment made available to me through Russian friends. The district authorities even gave me a photo identification card and monthly ration coupons for products in short supply. Three years later, when I retired, I was able to buy an apartment that had been built in the Khrushchev years. When it was torn down during Putin's presidency, I was given a new apartment at no cost. As you know, it's worth ten times what I paid for my first home sweet home in Russia."

"We're about to leave the reservoir," Zhanna said, looking at her watch. "I have more questions for you, but they'll have to wait. We need to prepare our guests for the landing at Irma."

Irma is a small rustic village where ships stop to give passengers a chance to stretch their legs, wander amongst log cabins built by summer residents, admire the church with its three golden cupolas, and contribute to the local economy by purchasing souvenirs at the flea market. The market is the first and last sight for tourists arriving and departing by ship.

No one had much to say about the village. It didn't take long to see the sights, the highlight of which was a man, oblivious to tourists, wielding an ax with strength and precision. He was putting the finishing touches on his log cabin. It was worth a picture or two.

What the group enjoyed most was the flea market. In the hour of leisure time that remained, the group went from stall to stall trying to decide what souvenirs to take back with them. The nesting dolls, the *matrëshki*, were the biggest drawing card. As Zhanna explained, the number of dolls in a set, one inside another, ranged from two to twenty-four. "A really rare set," she said, "could have as many as sixty dolls." The sets on display at the port were not rare, but that did not discourage customers. Neville opted for a set of six: Stalin, Khrushchev, Brezhnev, Gorbachev, Yeltsin, and Putin. More in demand were the traditional sets, dolls dressed in the style and colors of Russian legends and fairy tales.

Brisk business was also evident at tables selling lacquered boxes with common Russian motifs. John had one at home that showed Russian *troiki*, three-horse sleds, dashing through the snow in a circle. Further on were displays of jewelry. Peter was pleased to see that special attention was being given to necklaces and bracelets made of amber, the national gem of Lithuania. When Peter noticed Blanche admiring an amber brooch with its yellow, honey-like color, he explained that amber is washed up from the bottom of the Baltic Sea and has been collected on the shores since time immemorial.

"In the Lithuanian coastal city of Palanga," Peter told Blanche, "there is a museum with nothing but amber. Our tour doesn't take us to the Land of Amber, as Lithuania is sometimes called, but in St. Petersburg we'll see the Eighth Wonder of the World, the Amber Room. The original panels with over six tons of amber, backed with gold leaf, were stolen by the Germans during the Second World War, but the Amber Room has recently been reconstructed. It's magnificent. You'll see."

The flea market was also a cornucopia of fresh vegetables. There was no dearth of food on the ship, but several couples couldn't resist. The ship's next stop, Kizhi, would not be for another two days. Zhanna and John wanted to laugh but just smiled at passengers who boarded the ship with souvenirs in one hand and vegetables, especially carrots, in the other. "We have an expression," John whispered in Zhanna's ear, "To each his own. Or as the French say, *Chacun á son goût.*"

CHAPTER 7

O n its way north to Kizhi, the *Novikov Priboi* cruised White Lake, the Volga–Baltic Canal, and Lake Onega. Passengers were entertained by folk dancers in native dress and by concerts featuring a violinist and an accordion player. In addition to Russian language lessons by Zhanna, there was also a talk by John on Russian politics. John began with a question while crossing Lake Onega.

"Has anyone heard of Stieg Larsson?"

"Sure," said a voice from the back of the room. "He was a Swedish novelist. His trilogy about justice and morality was a bestseller everywhere."

"What's Larsson got to do with Russian politics?" Neville asked with a puzzled look on his face.

"It's got to do with revenge," John answered. "Like the author, his main characters never forget or forgive. Larsson once told a friend that to exact revenge is not only a right but also an absolute duty, even if it's unethical or perhaps illegal. The novels got me to thinking about revenge as a motive in Russian politics. That leads me to my next question. Has anyone heard of Aleksandr Rutskoi?"

After a long pause, an elderly man in the front row responded. "If I remember correctly, he was a Russian politician, a terrorist, who tried unsuccessfully to overthrow President Yeltsin in the early 1990s."

"If Yeltsin were alive today, you would get an A+ for that answer," John said. "When Yeltsin ordered tanks to fire on the Russian White House in October 1993, where Rutskoi and his supporters were entrenched, Yeltsin described the object of his attack as a citadel of terrorism."

"You're going to give us a different reading of events," Peter said with a knowing smile.

"Am I that obvious?" John asked rhetorically. "It's been said that I'm a bit contrarian. When I submitted a manuscript about Rutskoi not long after the storming of the White House, one reviewer said that it read like a propaganda eulogy straight out of the Stalinist era. A second reviewer wondered how I could find anything positive to say about a man who, in his opinion, would spend the rest of his life in prison for organizing mass disorder."

"What specifically did you say that struck such a negative chord with the reviewers?" Peter asked from his seat in the front row.

"When Yeltsin was elected President of the Russian Federation in 1991, he chose Rutskoi as his Vice-President. A Hero of the Soviet Union, Rutskoi was second only to Yeltsin in popularity. During the campaign Rutskoi stated that he was in agreement with Yeltsin eighty percent of the time, although he acknowledged some discord over tactics. In the ensuring months discord turned into serious disagreements about politics and economics. Has anyone heard of Jeffrey Sachs?"

"He was the Harvard professor and economist who advised Yeltsin," Neville said proudly, thinking of his own degree from Harvard. "Nowadays he's a professor at Columbia University and a frequent guest on a national news program."

"Right," John said. "Sachs, along with other Western economists, played a major role in Yeltsin's decision to bring capitalism to Russia through shock therapy. Rutskoi protested. He was opposed to foreigners telling Russia how to run its economy, and he wanted to restore law and order, which he felt shock therapy was undermining. Rutskoi went so far as to accuse the police of corruption, asserting that organized crime controlled forty percent of Russia's GNP. Rutskoi said that he had a suitcase full of evidence, although it was never produced."

"No wonder Yeltsin was upset," one listener said. "What did he do?"

"He established a special committee on crime and corruption, which proceeded to accuse Rutskoi of salting away three million dollars in a Swiss bank account. After an investigation in Zurich, Moscow's chief prosecutor stated that Rutskoi had no dollars in a Swiss account. Rutskoi was reminded of the NKVD, Stalin's secret police, while the prosecutor saw parallels with the McCarthy era in American politics. President Yeltsin suspended Rutskoi from his vice-presidential duties pending further investigation into the charges of corruption."

"Was there a final determination as to Rutskoi's guilt or innocence?" Peter asked.

"No," John answered. "The inquiry ended when Yeltsin dissolved the Russian parliament with a presidential decree. The Constitutional Court declared the decree a violation of the Russian constitution, and it approved a decision by the Russian parliament to elevate Rutskoi to the position of Acting President. The Court, too, was then dissolved by decree."

"Sounds like Yeltsin had numerous enemies, not just Rutskoi," someone in the audience remarked.

"Yeltsin was determined," John responded, "to establish a presidential form of government with a weak parliament, a cabinet of his choosing, and no vice-president. Rutskoi, hitherto a spokesman for moderation, wanted the locus of power to be in a democratically elected parliament with control over the executive branch of government. When parliament was cut off from all utilities and surrounded by police with razor wire, Rutskoi was forced into a union with extremists in the red-brown movement of nationalists. Led by General Makashov, extremists attacked the Mayor's Office and the Ostankino television station. They were defeated by an elite detachment of the police, whose Director told the Chief Justice to forget about a compromise solution to the escalating conflict. On October 4, 1993, tanks opened fire on the White House."

"But Rutskoi wasn't killed," an attentive listener commented.

"No," John said. "He surrendered and was put in prison. The Kremlin-controlled media vilified him as a cockroach and a traitor. Yeltsin stated that there would be no forgiveness for Rutskoi and other leaders of what Yeltsin called an armed revolt planned many months in advance. On this last point, the Director of the Federal Security Service (FSB) disagreed. A few days after the storming of the White House he stated publicly that the events of October 3-4 occurred spontaneously and were not in the plans of those in the White House. As Rutskoi told an Italian journalist, they couldn't control the actions of people with different ideological beliefs who flocked to defend the White House."

"Why didn't Yeltsin's forces just shoot Rutskoi after he was taken prisoner?" Neville asked. "Like what happened to Osama bin Laden. Over and done with."

"That's an interesting question," John replied. "Rutskoi had a telephone conversation with the Chief Justice during the siege, and in that conversation, which was taped and broadcast on Russian Radio Echo, Rutskoi claimed that Yeltsin and the Minister of the Interior had given orders not to take witnesses alive. Who knows? I certainly don't. What I do know is that Parliament passed a sweeping amnesty for participants in the events of August 1991 and October 1993. Rutskoi reentered politics and was elected Governor of the Kursk region with seventy-six percent of the popular vote. When he attended Yeltsin's burial in 2007, Rutskoi could not be coaxed by the press into negative statements about the deceased."

"Is Yeltsin's anointed successor, Putin, a believer in revenge?" Neville asked. "I remember reading in the *The Economist* about Putin's revanchism. The article said that the Kremlin holds a grudge against the tycoons."

"Unlike Yeltsin," John replied, "there is no evidence that Putin is a follower of Vladimir the Wise and his rules of revenge. On the other hand, we all probably have felt the desire to get even with someone. For Putin it was a few Russian oligarchs, or, as we call them, Russian business tycoons."

"One name pops up all the time," Peter said. "Not too long ago there was a full page piece in *The New York Times* about Khodorkovsky written by a fellow oligarch who moved to Israel. The émigré writes that Khodorkovsky, his friend, is a champion of democracy and freedom, not a man guilty of tax evasion, fraud, and money laundering. Why then is Khodorkovsky behind bars?"

"There is no simple answer," John said. "I would start with a meeting that Putin had with oligarchs soon after becoming president. He told them that they could keep their ill-gotten wealth from the Yeltsin years provided that they paid their taxes and stayed out of politics. Khodorkovsky, a billionaire and the richest man in Russia, refused to accept the rules laid down by Putin. Khodorkovsky made no bones about his belief that the most profitable business in Russia is politics and that he wanted to be a key player in that business. What followed was Khodorkovsky's arrest, his trial, his conviction, and his imprisonment."

"Was the trial fair?" Francis asked.

"A British journalist compared it to the show trials under Stalin. Khodorkovsky disclaimed personal responsibility for any violation of Russian law, although with respect to tax evasion he said that everyone was doing it. The Moscow court sentenced Khodorkovsky to seven years in prison. Western journalists cried foul, even though the European Court of Human Rights did not see political motivation behind Khodorkovsky's prosecution. Khodorkovsky continues to issue political statements from his prison cell in Siberia, which could very well explain why five years for money laundering have recently been added to the original sentence for fraud and tax evasion. Tow the line, or else, is Putin's message to oligarchs living in Russia."

"What about oligarchs who took their money and left Russia?" Neville asked. "In particular, what about Boris Berezovsky in the UK?"

"For those of you who haven't heard of Berezovsky," John said, "I should begin by saying that he rose from a car salesman to one of the richest men in Russia thanks to Yeltsin's crooked giveaway, euphemistically called the loans-for-shares program. When Berezovsky decided to flee the country he sold his shares in the most widely watched television network, ORT, for $170 million and his shares in the oil company Sibneft for $1.3 billion." John paused and chuckled.

"There's humor in getting rich overnight?" Francis asked.

"Black humor," John responded. "Berezovsky now claims that he was cheated when he sold his Sibneft shares to another Russian oligarch, Roman Abramovich, who owns the Chelsea Football Club but is domiciled in Russia. Berezovsky believes that he should have received $2.5 billion, not a mere $1.3 billion, for his shares. The two Russian oligarchs are duking it out in a London courtroom. *The Guardian* describes it as the pugnacious Berezovsky versus the diffident and media-shy Abramovich whose real interest is business, not politics."

"Would Berezovsky be sitting in a Russian prison if he had not fled the country?"

"Absolutely," John replied. "Like Khodorkovsky, he is unwilling to separate business from politics. Berezovsky freely admits that he uses business for political objectives."

"What are his objectives?" asked a man wearing a McLenin t-shirt bought as a souvenir at the Irma flea market.

"That's an easy one," John replied. "Berezovsky is on record as having said that it is not only acceptable but also necessary for the oligarchs to interfere directly in the Russian political process. He acknowledges that he is working to overthrow Putin by force and that he has spent more than $100 million in his campaign against Putin, the Russian government, and the Federal Security Service."

"I'll bet Putin would like to get his hands on Berezovsky," Neville said

"The Kremlin has sought, unsuccessfully, to have him extradited. Moscow would like to get Berezovsky into a Russian court to face charges similar to those brought against Khodorkovsky, but London refuses to extradite Berezovsky because he was granted political asylum in 2002. With respect to Berezovsky's call to arms against the Russian government, Britain's Crown Prosecution Service found insufficient evidence to charge him with incitement to terrorism."

"Why doesn't the Kremlin just poison him with polonium? That's what they did to Litvinenko," Neville said smugly.

"There are more questions than answers about Litvinenko's murder," John replied. "Who was behind the assassination? Like many people in the West, you point the finger of guilt at Putin. After Litvinenko was fired from the Federal Security Service in 1998 for having accused his superiors of corruption and a plot to assassinate Berezovsky, for whom he moonlighted, Litvinenko was charged with exceeding his authority by going public with his accusations. Although acquitted, Litvinenko fled the country. First to Turkey, where the U.S. Embassy refused to grant him political asylum, and then to the United Kingdom, where he eventually became a naturalized British citizen."

"Why kill him?" a skeptic in the audience asked. "That's a bit extreme, don't you think?"

"It's what Litvinenko did after he was granted asylum in the UK," John said. "Litvinenko accused the Kremlin of orchestrating the bombings of apartment buildings in 1999, the Moscow theater siege in 2002, and the Beslan school hostage crisis in 2004. Putin retaliated against Litvinenko, so the argument goes, with a dose of polonium-210. If true, why then is Litvinenko's sponsor and financier still alive?"

"You're talking about Berezovsky," Zhanna said with a smile, knowing what John thought of the oligarch who has been described by an advocate as ruthless and by an associate as megalomaniac.

"There has been one real, and one alleged, attempt to assassinate Berezovsky," John continued. "In 1994, a year after he entered President Yeltsin's inner circle, a bomb went off in Berezovsky's car, killing his chauffeur. Given Berezovsky's business and political interests in Chechnya, which was at war with Russia, it is likely that Chechen terrorists were responsible for the attack. In 2007 Scotland Yard arrested a Russian in London for plotting to assassinate Berezovsky. Lacking enough evidence to charge the Russian with any offense, he was deported to Russia, where he was identified as a Chechen mobster."

"Okay," Neville said, "Berezovsky is alive. Litvinenko is dead. You seem to be saying that both men would be dead if Putin were hell-bent on assassinating outspoken critics who live abroad as political exiles. Are you saying that the Kremlin is not responsible for Litvinenko's death?"

"That's my theory," John said. "A case can certainly be made that Berezovsky, not Putin, was a central figure in the assassination."

"That sounds far-fetched to me," Neville said. "You've already indicated that Berezovsky was Litvinenko's patron saint, providing him with money and a sanctuary in the UK."

"Initially, yes, because Litvinenko's allegations against Putin were useful in Berezovsky's quest for revenge. With time, however, Litvinenko's assertions bordered on the absurd and called into question his reliability. It is not easy to believe, for example, that Putin is a pedophile. Litvinenko had outlived his usefulness to Berezovsky. That may explain why Berezovsky ceased to support him financially. Litvinenko had to find another source of income."

"A real job?" The question from the audience evoked snickers and a few smiles from listeners who associated Russians with crime and corruption, not with legitimate business activities.

"In conversations with a doctoral candidate at the University of Westminster," John replied, "Litvinenko revealed that he hoped to sell an exposé about an unnamed Russian oligarch. If true and if the oligarch was Berezovsky, one need only recall what happened to Paul Klebnikov, an editor for *Forbes* magazine and a relentless critic of Berezovsky. In July 2004 Klebnikov was gunned down on the streets of Moscow. The case was never solved, although *The Wall Street Journal* wrote that the perpetrator's name was probably on the list of Russia's richest oligarchs prepared by Klebnikov and published in *Forbes* magazine two months before his murder."

"Interesting but not convincing," Neville said.

"How about another theory implicating Berezovsky in Litvinenko's death?" John asked good-naturedly. "Litvinenko's slow and agonizing death from poison, rather than a bullet to the head, remained front-page news around the world for months. In Britain the publicity campaign was essentially dictated and funded by Berezovsky. One way or another Berezovsky was determined to get revenge against Putin, who had won the battle for power and influence in Russian politics."

"On that note," Zhanna said, "let's break for coffee, cakes, and *pirogi*."

Neville spotted Francis sitting alone in the lounge by a window. "Mind if I join you?" he asked. "A few days ago you had a question for me about morality and ethics. Now it's my turn. Okay?"

"Of course, and it won't cost you a penny," Francis said with a welcoming smile. "If I were to guess, I'd say you're interested in something John said this morning about revenge."

"As a psychologist, would you agree with John that the desire to get even is a normal reaction?"

"Yes," Francis said, "but most people only think about revenge. I tell patients that it is useful to vent their anger by writing about it, perhaps in a diary, rather than letting it consume your everyday existence. I would love to have a session with Berezovsky. He's a classic example of what can go wrong when you seek an eye for an eye, a tooth for a tooth."

"I once acted out of a desire for revenge," Neville admitted. "I don't regret it. What do you think?"

"Before making a judgment," Francis said, "I would need to know the circumstances."

"Let's call it a privileged communication between doctor and client," Neville said lightheartedly. "You told me that your own lapse in judgment occurred during a divorce proceeding and that it was motivated by money. I, too, acted unethically during a divorce proceeding, but it had nothing to do with money. I just wanted to get even with the husband."

"What did he do to alienate you?"

"As you know, when I retired from the Foreign Service I was hired as an administrator and teacher at an American university. The husband in question was chair of my department for five years. He considered me less deserving than other members of the faculty, even though I have a B.A. from Harvard and was U.S. Ambassador to the Central African Republic. I wanted a regular appointment as a professor of political science, but the department voted against me. I hold the chairman personally responsible. I was permitted to teach undergraduate courses but only like an adjunct until the university decided to create a new rank, a professor of practice. That's what I am, but that's not what I want to be. The chairman's second wife gave me a chance to get back at her husband."

"You were friends?"

"No. I barely knew her, but one day she telephoned and said that she would like to talk with me and my wife about her husband. I was intrigued and invited her over for coffee on a Saturday morning."

"What was on her mind?"

"Much younger than her husband, she wanted out of the marriage and was seeking custody of their two daughters. Their marriage, several years after the death of his first wife, lasted a little over a decade. She was fishing for anything negative about her husband. She probably knew that I held a grudge against him. The opening came when she asked about the death of his first wife."

"What did she want to know?"

"She questioned the suicide of his first wife. She thought that it might have been murder. She had even gone to the District Attorney with her suspicions. She wanted my opinion. I knew that the wife had been in a psychiatric facility for several months just prior to her death, but I played along. Moody and I agreed that murder by her husband was a distinct possibility. She told her psychologist of our conversation, and his notes were introduced during the court proceedings."

"Did your support help the wife?"

"The divorce went through," Neville said, "but she didn't win the custody battle."

"In other words, you didn't get your revenge."

"Oh yes, I did. I didn't expect the murder charge to play a significant role in the divorce proceedings, but I was sure that the mere accusation would hang like a cloud over the chairman for years to come. My revenge was short-lived, however. Rayback died in Moscow after retiring from the university."

"Rayback?" Francis asked. "The grave in the Novodevichy cemetery?"

"Yes, why?"

"That was my court case, too," Francis said with an astonished look on his face. "You and I transgressed together."

"That's ancient history," Neville said. "No need to worry about the past."

CHAPTER 8

In the morning all eyes were focused on Kizhi, an island six kilometers long and one kilometer wide situated in Lake Onega not far from Petrozavodsk, the capital of the Karelian Republic. The island is a national open-air museum with close to a hundred wooden structures, many of which were moved to the island from various parts of Karelia in the 1950s. Tourists reach Kizhi on hydrofoils from Petrozavodsk or on cruise ships like the *Novikov Priboi*. The star attraction is Kizhi Pogost, a UNESCO World Heritage Site on the southern tip of the island consisting of two domed wooden churches and a bell tower built in the eighteenth century.

"Fantastic," said one passenger as the ship glided through shallow waters and reeds in its approach to Kizhi. "I've never seen so many domes on a single church." She pointed off to her right at the Transfiguration Church, the jewel of Kizhi Pogost with its domes cast in hues of gray and silver. Peals from the adjacent bell tower welcomed the new arrivals. Within minutes they would be on shore entering wooden structures that owed their longevity, in part, to the suppression of bacterial activity by virtue of the region's cool weather.

Inside the wooden fence surrounding Kizhi Pogost, the group approached the two churches and bell tower on foot along a dirt path. "Count the domes," someone said.

"Twenty-two on the Transfiguration Church, nine on the Church of the Intercession," Zhanna said. She knew that it would be hard to count the domes because of their number and because the dark colors created a seamless connection to the ancient wooden structures.

With bells still ringing, Zhanna led the group back to where they had entered the Pogost. "Now we're going to visit one of the two remaining settlements on Kizhi."

"Do a lot of people live on the island?" Moody asked.

"Very few," Zhanna replied, leading her followers across a meadow to the Yamka settlement with its eleven houses.

"Are the mushrooms on those trees edible?" Madge asked as they trudged along another dirt path.

"Some of them," Zhanna replied. "There are at least twenty different species of polypores on Kizhi. My mother used to say that an edible mushroom could be identified by tipping it over with a branch to make sure it didn't bleed a milky white substance."

"I'll stick to mushrooms from a store," Peter said, laughing. "My Lithuanian grandmother had a great recipe for chanterelles. Fry them chopped up in olive oil along with diced onion and garlic. Then add a little flour, cream or milk, and soy sauce with a dash of salt and white pepper."

"You're making me hungry," Francis said.

"Don't fret," Zhanna said with a smile. "I'm sure the ship's cook will have a delicious lunch ready for us after we tour one of Yamka's wooden houses, its two chapels, and the windmill."

No one was disappointed. As the *Novikov Priboi* glided slowly away from Kizhi, passengers stowed their cameras and headed down to the dining room for a tantalizing buffet luncheon. John chose a grilled salmon steak with fresh dill and a salad with herring, chopped beets, carrots, and potatoes. Although his plate was full, he couldn't resist the wild rice pancakes with local mushrooms, sour cream, and chives. "I hope no one falls asleep during my afternoon discussion," John said to Zhanna, whose plate also had enough food to produce a delayed soporific effect.

"I'll try not to snore," Zhanna joked. "Who would want to miss what you have to say about Karelia? I'm sure it will be at variance with the serene and tranquil image of life in Karelia that a visit to Kizhi conveys."

John began his afternoon presentation with a little history. "When the Soviet Union was formed, there were about a hundred different nationalities in the country. Lenin rejected the tsarist policy of russification, declaring war on Great Russian chauvinism. In 1923 he put his imprimatur on what was called 'nativization.' Territorial autonomy at four different levels was implemented, and non-Russian peoples were encouraged to use their native tongues in written as well as oral form. This policy opened the door to a golden decade for Russia's ethnic minorities."

"You're implying that 'nativization' ended in 1933," Neville remarked quizzically, "but we just visited an island in the Karelian Republic."

"Territorial entities still exist," John explained. "What came to an end was the emphasis on native language utilization. Stalin, a Georgian, reinstituted Great Russian chauvinism. As Lenin warned in his notes on the nationality question, there is nothing worse than a russified non-Russian."

"Is Russian the official state language in Karelia?" Neville asked.

"It is today, but it hasn't always been like that. When 'nativization' was proclaimed, Russian and Finnish became the state languages in Karelia."

"Why Finnish?" someone asked. "Are there that many Finns living in Karelia?"

"Let me start by saying that the language question in Karelia was much more complicated than in other parts of the Soviet Union. When the Karelian republic was established in 1923, Russians constituted about fifty-five percent of the population. Karelians were in second place with forty-three percent. Bringing up the rear with less than two percent of the population were the Finns."

"I'm puzzled," someone said. "Why wasn't Karelian declared the second language along with Russian? What gave the Finnish minority so much clout? Finland's long border with Karelia?"

"Good questions," John replied, "No simple answers. First, Karelian was not a written language. In other parts of the Soviet Union some sixty literary languages were developed in support of 'nativization.' Why not do the same for Karelians? The answer is that Karelian speech had numerous dialects. The language spoken in the north was heavily influenced by Finnish. In central parts of Karelia, the influence of Finnish was less apparent. It was almost non-existent in the south, where Russian influence was strong.

"The decision to make Finnish, not Karelian, the second state language also had a personal element. After the Finnish Civil War of 1918 many of the defeated 'reds' sought refuge in the Soviet Union. Among them was a moderate socialist, Edvard Gylling, who had been a member of the Finnish Parliament for ten years as well as chairman of the Parliament's Board of Overseers for the Bank of Finland. In May 1920 he discussed the formation of a Karelian autonomous republic with Lenin, who gave his approval to the plan submitted by Gylling. Also influential was Kustaa Rovio, who as chief of police in the Finnish capital, Helsinki, provided Lenin with a safe haven from the Russian Provisional government in the summer of 1917. Rovio, first secretary of the Karelian communist party for six years, wrote that if Finnish had not been made the second state language, alongside Russian, the formation of an autonomous republic for Karelians would have been nonsensical."

"You said that 'nativization' came to an end in 1933," Neville remarked. "What happened to Gylling and Rovio? I assume they didn't become Heroes of the Soviet Union."

"In 1935 Gylling lost his job as chief executive of the state apparatus, and Rovio was removed as party secretary. Rovio's replacement, a Leningrad *apparatchik*, charged that Russian in Karelia was being undermined by the emphasis on Finnish. He also said that it was imperative to give Karelians in the republic their own written language. The new prime minister was by ethnic background a Tver Karelian, a predictor of what was on the horizon. In 1931 a literary language in the Latin alphabet had been developed for thousands of Karelians living just northwest of Moscow in the Tver (Kalininskaia) region. In 1937 it was announced that a literary language using the Cyrillic alphabet had been created for all Karelians. Finnish-language publications were banned. A newspaper in Karelian appeared, but, as noted by central authorities, Karelians couldn't understand the language. Once again, it was Russian for everybody."

"Back to Gylling and Rovio," Neville persisted. "I'll bet Stalin put them in their place."

"Two years after losing their state and party positions, both men left Karelia and were permitted to live in Moscow," John replied. "But they soon became victims of the Great Purge. They were arrested in the summer of 1937, accused of being traitors, turncoats, loathsome vipers, and agents of German–Finnish fascism. After that, it was pure speculation. Some said that Gylling died in 1942, while others claimed that he died in 1944 just south of Moscow in Tula. During the Brezhnev era, one of Gylling's closest friends said that no one really knows when and where he died. Rovio's fate was also a mystery.

"It was not until 2002 that the truth was revealed with publication of documents released to the Memorial Society from the Archive of the President of the Russian Federation. Known as Stalin's Lists (*Spiski Stalina*), the fate of 44,500 individuals on 383 lists became known. On April 19, 1938, Rovio's execution by shooting (*rasstrel*) was approved by Stalin, Molotov, Kaganovich, and Zhdanov. On June 10, 1938, Stalin and Molotov approved a category one sentence for Gylling, too, a bullet in the back of the head. During the Yeltsin era, one of Stalin's executioners demonstrated on national television how the sentences were carried out."

"Gruesome!" Moody exclaimed.

"Other revelations had been made previously by Khrushchev," John continued. "He shocked delegates to the Twentieth Party Congress with a condemnation of Stalin for committing crimes against the nation and the party. Khrushchev referred to cruel repression, including torture and death, inflicted by Stalin not only on politically defeated communists like Bukharin but also on 'honest and innocent' communists. Khrushchev announced that posthumous rehabilitations were underway. Awards would be returned, and there would be monetary compensation for damages inflicted on innocent victims and members of their families. A few months after the congress, Gylling and Rovio were officially rehabilitated by the General Secretary of the Finnish Communist Party."

"Perhaps it's time for a short coffee break," Zhanna suggested to the audience. "I'm sure John would like a little caffeine before he continues with his depressing narrative of life in Karelia under Stalin."

When everyone was again seated, coffee cups in hand, John began with a familiar name. "You've all heard of Solzhenitsyn, and perhaps some of you have even read *The Gulag Archipelago*. During the first of Stalin's Five Year Plans, two forced labor camp systems under Moscow's control were set up in Karelia. Solzhenitsyn traces the origins of the GULAG to a camp of 'special purpose' located in northern Karelia on the Solovetsky archipelago. In existence for ten years, 1929–1939, this camp system on the White Sea was the worst of the worst. It was not uncommon for prisoners on the main Solovetsky island to be tied to trees, naked, in both winter and summer. The bodies either froze or were eaten by mosquitoes. Nowadays the archipelago is a tourist attraction."

"Morbid fascination?" Francis asked.

"In part, yes," John replied. "There are tall crosses marking mass graves, and there is a small museum with exhibits from the camp. On the other hand, the islands are gorgeous if one doesn't think about what is buried beneath wild blueberry fields and awesome birch trees. White beluga whales swimming close to shore in the summer's midnight sun are also a sight to be seen. The main attraction, however, is the 16th century Solovetsky monastery surrounded by massive walls of granite and home to a white cathedral with silver domes."

"The land is a holy place for Solovetsky monks," Zhanna interjected. "After decades of banishment, they returned to the archipelago. They are not thrilled by entrepreneurs who want to open the islands to tourism. Without explanation, cruise ships from Europe are sometimes denied permission to dock."

Returning to his theme, John moved on to the second camp system in Karelia. "Solovetsky prisoners from camp three were transferred in 1931 to Stalin's first major project constructed with forced labor, a canal enabling ships to move from the Baltic to the White Sea. The canal begins about seventy-five miles north of Kizhi, at a village called Povenets, and ends at the city of Belomorsk on the White Sea. The total distance is about seventy-five miles, thirty of which required construction by prisoners with picks and shovels. The project was completed four months ahead of schedule in the summer of 1933. There is a monument at Povenets for prisoners who perished during construction of the *Belomorkanal*, and a smaller memorial at Belomorsk, where the canal enters the White Sea."

"Human life didn't mean a thing to Stalin," Neville commented. "Industrialization at any cost."

"No one knows for sure how many prisoners died while working on the Stalin White Sea-Baltic Canal," John said. "Thousands for sure. But the BBLag, as this system was called, fared better than other GULAG camps. A propaganda poster instilled hope for those working on the canal. The poster was titled 'Canal Army Soldier,' and it promised a reduced sentence through 'hot' physical labor. The camp newspaper called the process *perekovka*, a 're-forging' of prisoners."

"Were prisoners actually rewarded with early release?" Neville asked, shaking his head in disbelief.

"None that I know of," John replied. "What did happen, though, was that following completion of the *Belomorkanal* many workers were transferred south to work on the Moscow-Volga Canal. As far as Karelia is concerned, another chapter in its painful history was just around the corner. On November 30, 1939, the Soviet Union went to war with Finland over Karelian territory."

At least one person in the audience was puzzled. "Aside from a long border with Karelia, what interest does Finland have in Karelia?"

"Simple," John replied. "Ever since the days of Peter the Great, important parts of Karelia had been part of Finland. Finnish Karelia included much of the Isthmus between Lake Ladoga and the Gulf of Finland. In Soviet eyes the border was dangerously close to Leningrad. Stalin wanted to move the border further away from the city. In negotiations with the Finnish government, Stalin said that it was impossible to move Leningrad but that the border could be changed to provide more security for the city without harming Finland's vital interests.

"The chief Finnish negotiator understood the need for concessions, but his efforts at conciliation and moderation, greeted coolly at home by many politicians, were insufficient to resolve the impasse between Moscow and Helsinki. The Soviet Union proceeded to launch a land, sea, and air attack on Finland. After the commencement of hostilities, Moscow announced the formation of a Democratic People's Government of Finland.

"Located on the Karelian Isthmus sixty kilometers from Leningrad, this puppet government was headed by Otto W. Kuusinen. Kuusinen, like his compatriot, classmate, and friend Edvard Gylling, had been a member of the Finnish parliament for a decade before seeking refuge in Soviet Russia after defeat in the Finnish Civil War. During Gylling's tenure as prime minister of the Karelian Autonomous Republic, 1923-1935, Kuusinen was a high ranking functionary in the Communist International."

"The League of Nations reacted quickly," Neville commented, remembering his diplomatic history. "The Soviet Union was thrown out of the organization by virtue of Article 16 of the Covenant."

"But no one stepped forward with military assistance," John said. "Surprisingly, it was not a quick victory for Soviet troops. The world watched from the sidelines as the Red Army suffered enormous losses. Prone to exaggeration, Khrushchev wrote in his memoirs that the number of dead was a million. If true, this would give substance to a Finnish wartime ditty: 'They are so many, our country is so small. Where will we bury them all?' Finnish politicians were intoxicated by early military victories, but reality began to sink in. On March 12, 1940, a Peace Treaty was signed in Moscow, ending the Winter War."

"No doubt Moscow got what it wanted," one listener opined.

"Finland lost about thirty-five thousand square kilometers of territory," John replied, "including its second largest city, now called Vyborg. After the Peace Treaty the Autonomous Republic of Karelia was elevated to the status of a Union Republic headed by Otto Kuusinen."

"I guess Kuusinen finally got revenge on the country that had rejected him," Neville said. "It must have felt good after festering for so long."

"That's debatable," John responded. "Kuusinen's second wife, embittered by thirteen years in the GULAG with no intervention by her husband, argues in her memoirs that Kuusinen hated Finland and wanted revenge. On the other hand, Kuusinen is on record as having condemned individuals who harbor feelings of bitterness, hate, and revenge."

"What about the Finns living in Karelian lands that were ceded to the Soviet Union?" Peter asked, remembering the refugee status of his parents after the Soviet occupation of the Baltic States in the summer of 1940.

"Some 450,000 Karelian refugees were resettled in various parts of Finland," John responded. "It's fair to say that they were bitter. Like many Finns, they dreamed of revenge. The opportunity came when Hitler decided to launch Operation Barbarossa against the Soviet Union. He had no problem convincing the Finnish government to permit the stationing of German troops on Finnish soil, in Lapland, and to give the Wehrmacht transit rights to northern Norway. When Germany attacked the Soviet Union on June 22, 1941, there were 200,000 German troops in the north. On that day Hitler declared that German forces in Norway were standing together (*im bunde*) with Finnish troops."

"Why, then, did Finns call it a defensive war?" Neville asked.

"At first glance it looked defensive," John replied. "It was not until June 26th, one day after Soviet air attacks, that the Finnish Parliament proclaimed a state of war. A member of the Cabinet's Foreign Affairs Committee has acknowledged, however, that Finland was prepared to launch its own attack in early July if the Soviet Union had not taken the initiative. Finnish politicians were convinced that Germany would defeat the Soviet Union. This mistaken belief was poignantly expressed in a newspaper article after a month of fighting. The Speaker of the Finnish Parliament wrote that the German army was crushing Finland's treacherous enemy and that Finland's gloomy Winter War (*Talvisota*) was now a Continuation War (*Jatkosota*) as bright as summer with victory a certainty."

"In short," Neville added, "Finland was Germany's ally."

"Not exactly," John said. "Finland considered itself a cobelligerent with Germany against a common enemy but with an agenda of its own. Finns wanted to regain the lands that they had lost in the Winter War. That goal was achieved within a matter of months. Finnish troops then moved further into Karelia repossessing former territory 'with interest,' as one Finnish politician put it. The capital of Soviet Karelia soon fell to Finnish troops, forcing Otto Kuusinen and his protégé Iurii Andropov, both of whom would later become members of the CPSU Politburo, to flee north to Belomorsk on the White Sea.

"Finnish politicians drew the line when asked by Hitler to complete a circle around Leningrad. Finnish troops halted their advance on the Isthmus some fifteen miles from the city. As one member of the Finnish Cabinet said, Russia would never forgive Finland for helping Germany capture its Window on the West. This decision by the Finnish government made it possible for Moscow to supply Leningrad over what was called the Ice Road, three tracks from a newly constructed harbor on the southwestern tip of Lake Ladoga to three destinations on the southeastern shore. Despite blizzards and thin ice, more than 400 three-ton trucks were on the road every day in the winter of 1941-1942. When Soviet troops broke through along the shore of Lake Ladoga in January 1943, Leningrad was no longer completely dependent on the Ice Road for food and supplies. Eventually the 900-day siege came to an end."

"But the war dragged on," Neville said.

"For Germany and the Soviet Union," John responded. "Finland, on the other hand, was eager to exit the war as quickly as possible. In the summer of 1944 the Finnish President resigned and was replaced by Marshal Gustaf Mannerheim, the one person who commanded enough respect and trust at home to lead Finland out of the war. The obligations spelled out in the Armistice Agreement of September 1944 were severe but nonetheless accepted by a new team of Finnish representatives. In addition to major territorial losses, Finland was required to pay exorbitant reparations over a six-year period in the form of commodities, primarily ships and machinery. Finland was also obligated to disarm German forces on Finnish soil. As Germany's Twentieth Alpine Army slowly withdrew from Lapland, parts of northern Finland were destroyed as payback for betrayal in the war against the Soviet Union."

"What about refugees?" Peter asked.

"History repeats itself," John began. "As I mentioned earlier, nearly half a million refugees were resettled in various parts of Finland after the Winter War. During the Continuation War almost two-thirds of these refugees returned to their Karelian homes. In 1944, when victory turned into defeat, there was a massive exodus of refugees back to Finland. In a radio speech on the eve of the March 1945 parliamentary elections, the Finnish Prime Minister turned his back on retribution and vengeance. He stated bluntly that Finland needed a new foreign policy and that the words 'hereditary enemy' had to be forgotten once and for all."

"I am reminded of an ancient Jewish proverb," Zhanna said as John concluded his remarks about Karelian history. "If you live to seek revenge, dig a grave for two. That's something to think about as we approach St. Petersburg tomorrow morning along the Svir River, peaceful now with idyllic cottages on its banks but a ferocious battleground during the Great Patriotic War."

CHAPTER 9

"Good morning," Zhanna said to the ship's passengers as they seated themselves for breakfast. "You may have loved Moscow, but you will be overwhelmed by St. Petersburg. It's my favorite city."

"I'm partial to Moscow," John interjects. "I am reminded of the rivalry between two Australian cities, Sydney and Melbourne. If you've seen the play *Emerald City*, you know what I mean."

With a smile on her face, Zhanna continued. "After breakfast I'll guide you to famous landmarks along the Neva River. Wear comfortable shoes. Then we'll go by bus to Pushkin (*Tsarskoe Selo*), southwest of the city, for lunch at a wooden dacha followed by a visit to the Palace of Catherine the Great. In the evening we have a special treat in store for you. An exclusive performance by Mariinsky ballet stars in the Hermitage Theatre."

First stop on the morning tour was a huge statue of Peter the Great mounted on a horse by the Neva River. "It was a monument from Catherine the Great honoring the Tsar who had opened a Window on the West, St. Petersburg. Not the greatest place for a city," Zhanna added.

"It looks good to me," Neville commented.

"The swampy marshes along the river led to periodic flooding of the city," Zhanna replied. "That was the theme of a poem by Pushkin, *The Bronze Horseman*, that was put to music by Glière. The ballet was first performed in the Kirov theater on the 150th anniversary of Pushkin's birth. It's a tragic love story about a young woman who drowns when the Neva overflows. The woman's lover goes insane with grief and shakes his fist at the Bronze Horseman. The statue comes to life and chases the lover to his death."

"I would like to add two vignettes," John said. "I saw the ballet at the Kirov theater many years ago, on my first trip to the Soviet Union. The staging was fantastic. The simulated flooding caused

CONFESSIONS & PAYBACK ON A VOLGA CRUISE

people in the audience to gasp. Nowadays the Bronze Horseman stays put and receives flowers from newlyweds. During the Yeltsin years of shock therapy I saw one down-and-out individual gather up the fresh flowers, stuff them in a bag, and head off for what he hoped would be a quick sale around the corner."

From the Bronze Horseman to St. Isaacs Cathedral was a five-minute walk. "It's the third largest domed cathedral in the world," Zhanna remarked. "When we get to the top of the Cathedral, you'll get a remarkable view of Palace Square with its towering red granite column topped off with an angel holding a cross. Palace Square was the scene of Bloody Sunday in 1905 and the October Revolution in 1917. In recent times it has been the setting for international concerts. The Rolling Stones, Elton John, Madonna, Sting, and Shakira."

Looking down from the top of the Cathedral, John called attention to another landmark. The Astoria Hotel. "It's considered one of the most romantic hotels in the world."

"Have you ever stayed there?" Madge asked with a twinkle in her eye.

"Before I get into that," John said with a smile, "let me mention a few of the famous guests. Margaret Thatcher and Tony Blair. Fedor Shaliapin, the renowned Russian singer whose grave you saw in Moscow. And Isadora Duncan, considered by many the creator of modern dance. She considered classical ballet ugly and against nature. An American by birth and a citizen of the Soviet Union, she lived half her life in Europe. During her last tour in the United States, on stage in Boston, she waved a red scarf and bared her breast proclaiming 'This is red! So am I!' Duncan's personal life was flamboyant and tragic. She was only fifty years old when her long silk scarf got entwined in the wheel of a French friend's Amil touring car. She was yanked to the pavement and broke her neck. Her ashes are in a Paris cemetery."

"Okay, John, now it's back to your story," Madge prompted.

"It was long, long ago that I stayed in the Astoria. Exciting, but not romantic. The *Porgy & Bess* troupe had just arrived from Berlin. I met the manager while having breakfast, and he invited me to have supper with the cast. In my diary I wrote that they were charming people. My comrade-in-arms, so to speak, was Al Hoosman, the understudy for Crown, the violent and possessive lover of Bess. Hoosman was huge. At one time he ranked number eight in the heavyweight fight division. He had been a sparmate with Joe Louis, and he liked to talk about what he called the crooked fight game."

"How did Russians relate to the black actors?" Francis asked. "Hostile?"

"On the contrary," John said. "One evening I asked Hoosman to have a drink with me. As we were looking for a table, two Russians ushered us over to their table. They refused to let us pay for the vodka and wine that we consumed. Other Russians joined us around midnight. They were fascinated by two Americans, one black and one white. In those days we certainly were an oddity on the Soviet scene."

"Did the Russians ask about race relations in America?"

"Yes," John replied. "And I have to say that Hoosman answered the questions honestly but diplomatically. It was a memorable evening for everyone. It's a pity that I didn't keep in touch with Hoosman."

"*Porgy & Bess* is on Broadway right now," Peter said. "*Time Magazine* ranks it the #1 musical of the year."

"Even without Hoosman!" John chuckled, remembering his black giant from yesteryear.

After exiting the Cathedral, Zhanna led the group past the Astoria Hotel over to a golden archway off Nevsky Prospekt that is the entrance to Palace Square. "What you see behind that towering red granite column," Zhanna explained, "is the Hermitage Museum ensemble with over three million works of art and artifacts. It's an ornate complex of six green baroque buildings with splashes of gold trim. The largest building, which we are facing, is the Winter Palace. It was the official royal residence until the February revolution of 1917, which brought Aleksandr Kerensky's Provisional Government to power. Kerensky's government held its meetings in a small room, the Malachite Room, on the other side of the building, facing the Neva River. It was in an adjacent dining room that members of the Provisional Government were arrested by the bolsheviks in October 1917."

"They were probably shot," someone in the group ventured.

"Most were imprisoned in the Peter & Paul Fortress," John replied. "Kerensky, disguised as a female nurse, escaped from the Winter Palace when it was stormed by the bolsheviks."

"Tell them about your meeting with Kerensky," Zhanna prompted.

"Well, it wasn't in 1917," John laughed. "It was at a luncheon in the States back in the 1960s. Kerensky was already in his eighties, too old to remember much from the past. In a few years I'll know all about that!"

Zhanna rolled her eyes, while others smiled. "Next stop is the Church of Blood," John continued.

"That's a strange name for a church," an elderly man said, crossing himself.

"The church," John explained, "was built on the site where the Tsar who freed the serfs, Alexander II, was assassinated when a bomb was hurled at his carriage by revolutionaries dissatisfied with the pace and scope of the Tsar's reforms. I am reminded of Gorbachev, whose pace was too slow for liberals and too fast for conservatives. Just before his resignation from the Soviet presidency, Gorbachev stated that he knew of no happy reformers."

Zhanna led the group up Nevsky Prospekt and over to a side street that leads to the Griboedov Canal. She stopped by a cast iron fence on the embankment, beyond which were the blue and gold beveled domes of the most photographed church in St. Petersburg, the Church of Blood.

"If you think the outside of the Church is beautiful," Zhanna said, "wait until you see what's inside. Believe it or not, there are 7,500 square meters of mosaics. No other church in the world can match it."

While tourists from the *Novikov Priboi* were walking from one artistic gem to another, John was scribbling notes in his diary.

"What's up?" Zhanna asked. "Are you working for the FSB?" They both laughed.

"I'm jotting down reactions to the mosaics on the walls and the ceiling of this fabulous church."

"How about enlightening me," Zhanna said.

"Of course," John said. "Superb. Spectacular. Unbelieveable. Gorgeous. Breathtaking. Stunning. Magical. Awesome. Unforgettable."

"What more could one ask for?" Zhanna asked.

"We'll see what our group says when we get to *Tsarskoe Selo*," John answered.

After a stop at the ship to freshen up, the travelers boarded a bus for the ride to what is now called Pushkin Village, twenty-five kilometers southwest of St. Petersburg. Lunch at *Dacha Terem* would be followed by a tour of the Amber Room in the Palace of Catherine the Great.

The restaurant was an impressive wooden building with four peaks and a majestic tower. Surrounding the structure was a garden with giant green ferns and tall sunflowers mixed in with red, pink, and yellow gladiolas. Unlike three gypsies in the courtyard, who were chased away by a Cossack-looking keeper of the gate, the Americans and Canadians from the *Novikov Priboi* were greeted warmly and ushered into the foyer of *Dacha Terem*.

The ambiance was definitely old-fashioned Russian hospitality. The entryway had a table with flowers, a samovar, and a bottle of vodka with a *matrëshka* doll observing from a niche in the wall. The luncheon guests were immediately serenaded by a quartet dressed in colorful folk costumes. It was not long before everyone was in motion to the beat of music from an accordion, a balalaika, a tambourine, and castinettes. Festivities then moved upstairs to a long table in a small dining room with fur pelts hanging on log walls and a stuffed bear and wolf standing in corners by the window overlooking the garden.

The delicacies on the table were interspersed with bottles of vodka and wine. It didn't take long before eager hands began to unscrew bottle tops. Neville led the pack. After one too many glasses of the green snake, he thought that a waitress was flirting with him. She wasn't. She did her best to remain cool when Neville pinched her derrière.

"No more vodka," Moody cautioned with trepidation. "You're a diplomat, not a Don Juan. Behave yourself," she whispered.

Unlike a similar indiscretion in the Russian Parliament by Boris Yeltsin, this incident was not filmed for posterity. Neville's shipmates were too busy clacking small castinettes and tapping their fingers on the table in consonance with a final song by the restaurant's quartet.

After a round of applause for the *maitre d'* and his staff, the revelers went outside for a breath of fresh air before boarding their bus. Some of the patrons wandered over to the garden to admire and touch the waist-high gladiolas. Others watched a Canadian hockey fan, Bill, twist and turn in order to show off the red, blue, and white jersey that he was wearing.

"What does it say?" Francis asked. "I don't read Russian."

"On the front it says 'Russia.' On the back it says 'Yashin #19.' Yashin was a star in the National Hockey League when he played for the Ottawa Senators. He eventually returned to Russia."

"Why would he do that?" Francis asked.

"He got into contract disputes. He wanted more money."

"I can relate to that," Francis said without thinking.

"All aboard for Catherine's Palace!" Zhanna interrupted, hustling people to an Intourist bus with its engine already running. "You don't want to miss the Eighth Wonder of the World. I'll let your fellow traveler, Peter Krukas, explain while we are en route."

"As some of you know," Peter began, "I have an art gallery in New York City on Madison Avenue. Because of my Lithuanian heritage, I keep on permanent display many pieces of amber, Lithuania's national gem. The yellow, honey-like color of Baltic amber is seductive. On a visit to Dresden in the eighteenth century, Peter the Great received a special gift from the Prussian King. It was known as the Amber Room. Its pure amber panels, mirrors, and precious stones were a beauty to behold, a treasure trove that was stolen by the Nazis from Catherine's Palace in *Tsarskoe Selo* and transported to an unknown location in Germany. What you will soon see is a replica of the Amber Room."

"Why weren't the Germans forced to return the original Amber Room at the end of the war?" Bill asked.

"To date no one knows where the Nazis put the Amber Room. Treasure hunters believe it is buried somewhere in the labyrinth of underground storage caverns built by the Germans at the end of the war. German and Lithuanian search teams have spent years looking for the Amber Room. In 2008 a German team claimed to have discovered it in a deep, man-made cavern near the border with the Czech Republic. There has been no confirmation, and I had serious doubts from the very beginning."

"Why?" John asked.

"Two reasons," Peter replied. "First, the German treasure hunters based their conclusion on the discovery of two metric tons of gold in a cavern. The Amber Room had six tons of amber, but very little gold. Second, amber is a fossil resin that decays in the dark. It would not have survived sixty years underground."

As the bus approached the blue façade of Catherine's Palace with its white columns and gold trim, Peter added, "Believe me, you will love the replica of the Amber Room. Russian craftsmen worked on it for nearly two decades, with financial donations from Germany."

Inside the Palace it seemed like there was gold everywhere, even in the dining room with its traditional Russian ceramic stove of blue extending from floor to ceiling. Gold leaf was visible at the group's final destination, too, but it was the amber that captivated the viewers.

"Those panels and mosaics must be worth a fortune," Francis whistled.

"Maybe three hundred million dollars," Peter replied, "but for me it's the beauty that counts." The group seemed to agree. Cameras worked overtime, photographing panels that are masterpieces of baroque art and widely regarded as among the world's most important art treasures.

"It's been quite a day," Blanche said to John as the group walked back to the bus for the return trip to the city.

"There's more to come," John said. "This evening we are taking you to the Hermitage Theatre, built by Catherine the Great. Seven Mariinsky ballet stars will perform to the music of Tchaikovsky, Saint-Saens, Puni, Adan, and Minkus. The Dying Swan will no doubt be familiar to many of you, but my favorite, Don Quixote, is less well-known. Since it's a private performance for our group, there is no prohibition on cameras."

"It reminds me of an amphitheater," Peter said to Madge as they entered the building. "It's breathtaking," he continued as he looked at the columns, decorated with colored marble, and at the statues of Apollo and the Nine Muses in niches.

"The bas-relief portraits above the niches," Zhanna explained, "are famous musicians and poets."

Soon the lights dimmed. The orchestra began to play, and the curtain slowly rose. It was the same curtain used in November 1785 for the ceremonial opening of the Hermitage Theatre. In the center of the curtain was a state symbol dating back to the 15th century, a two-headed eagle with gold crowns looking east and west.

The performance began with *White Adagio*, followed by *Esmeralda*, the *Nutcracker*, *Don Quixote*, and a pas-de-deux from *Le Corsaire* and *Sleeping Beauty*. Last but not least was the *Dying Swan*, performed by one of the renowned classical solo dancers in the Mariinsky corps de ballet.

"Isadora Duncan would not have appreciated Olga Sazanova," John said to Zhanna, who was sitting next to him, "but listen to the applause."

"Now it's our turn to go on stage." Zhanna nudged John.

"Not to dance, I hope," John answered, knowing full well that he and Zhanna were about to present each of the seven dancers with a bouquet of flowers while the audience continued its applause for an extraordinary evening.

As Zhanna led her charges to the Intourist bus that would take them back to the *Novikov Priboi*, she turned to John with a smile on her face. "There's a surprise waiting for you at the bar in the *Evropeiskaia* Hotel. I'll meet you there in about an hour, after I have tucked our guests in for the night."

John was puzzled as he walked up Nevsky Prospekt to the hotel, where he had once, long ago, stayed in a suite with a jacuzzi. He didn't need directions to get to the bar, but he had no idea what the surprise might be until he felt a tap on his shoulder. It was Zhanna's father, Viktor.

"This is a pleasant surprise," John said. "What brings you to St. Petersburg?"

"I couldn't resist spending an evening with my daughter and her beloved non-suitor, my dear American friend."

"Stop pulling my leg," John said in jest. "What's the real reason for your trip?"

"After Zhanna's tour of the Novodevichy cemetery," Viktor explained, "she told me that one member of the group was surprised when they came to the grave of my friend Michael Rayback. She gave me a list of the passengers, with one name highlighted. I recognized that name, Neville Ogleby, as well as the name of an American psychologist, Francis Pickle. Michael had nothing but contempt for both men. He resented what they did during his divorce proceedings."

"How do you know all this?" John asked.

"I met Michael by chance long ago during one of his many trips to the Soviet Union. Over the years we became fast friends. We had a lot in common." Viktor laughed.

"What's so funny?"

"Like Michael, I was often abroad at a time when foreign travel for Russian citizens was restricted. The Cold War, you know. When Michael applied for his first visa to the Soviet Union, he was told by the Russian Consul in Helsinki that tourists to his country were few and far between. Our travels abroad made us both suspect. In fact, during Michael's divorce his wife expressed her belief that Michael was a spy. But she didn't know which side he was spying for, Russia or the United States. After his divorce, Michael moved to Moscow and we saw each other on a regular basis. We had no secrets from each other, including the details of his divorce."

"Okay," John said. "Tell me. What did Ogleby and Pickle do to alienate Rayback and provoke you?"

"Michael's wife, Claudia, gave Ogleby an opportunity to get back at her husband. She was convinced that Michael had murdered his first wife for another woman, even though the coroner's report concluded that the death was a suicide from a drug overdose. In testimony presented to the court, Ogleby was more than willing to agree with Claudia's scenario."

"Why would he do that?" John asked, a puzzled look on his face.

"Revenge," Viktor replied succinctly and without hesitation. "After retiring from the Foreign Service, Ogleby was given an adjunct teaching position in a university department chaired by Michael Rayback. Ogleby wanted a regular professorial rank, but the department voted against giving him the status that he thought he deserved. He held Michael personally responsible for the negative vote and wanted to get even. By agreeing with Claudia, Ogleby knew that Michael's reputation would be tarnished forever, at least in the minds of some people, regardless of the facts."

"What about Francis Pickle?" John asked.

"The child custody evaluation report that he submitted to the court was distorted, even falsified, in favor of the mother." Viktor shook his head.

"Another case of revenge?" John asked.

"Not at all," Viktor replied. "Money, pure and simple. Pickle was going through bankruptcy proceedings, and he had no qualms about accepting a bribe from Claudia in return for an evaluation asserting that Michael met the criteria for a Narcissistic Personality Disorder. Pickle's conclusion was that Claudia should be designated the custodial parent."

"Rayback must have been furious," John said.

"He was," Viktor responded. "He challenged the competency of Pickle in a complaint filed with a regional branch of the Office of Professional Discipline. He was told that his complaint had merit but that it went beyond the scope of the Office. The senior investigator recommended that Michael pursue the matter with the Ethics Committee of the American Psychological Association. Michael proceeded to file a complaint with the Association, arguing that Pickle had not maintained a reasonable level of awareness of current scientific and professional information in his field as required by the APA's Ethical Principles and Code of Conduct. Four months later Michael received a response from the APA. As the letter said, it was not the outcome that Michael expected. An ethics case against Pickle would not be opened. Michael did not lose custody of his children, but he was still branded with the same personality disorder ascribed to Hitler, Stalin, and Saddam Hussein. Perhaps now is the time for payback. Do you believe in revenge, John?"

"What's up?" Zhanna asked, arriving in time to catch the tail end of her father's conversation with John. "Sounds like a conspiracy—payback and revenge."

"We were talking about what Ogleby and Pickle did to my friend Michael Rayback. You know the story, and you know how I feel about revenge. An eye for an eye, a tooth for a tooth. Perhaps John disagrees."

"I'm not a vengeful person," John said, "but I don't believe in turning the other cheek. As my wife once put it, don't get on my wrong side."

"Would you do anything unethical or illegal?" Zhanna asked.

"No," John replied. "I'm more like Don Quixote, tilting at windmills. I fight battles, often unwinnable or futile, in pursuit of justice. As you know, I was once considered a security risk. When the Freedom of Information Act became law, I made a request for information about my case. As *The New York Times* recently reported, quoting a top official, some cases can drag on for so long that the requests are from people who are dead. That was my experience."

"But you're not dead," Zhanna joked. "What did you get?"

"I initiated requests to the FBI and to the CIA. I heard from the CIA nine months after filing my request. I was told there were no records available to me. I filed an appeal, which was rejected five years later. After waiting four years to hear from the FBI, I received a letter asking whether I was still interested in the material given the lengthy time that had elapsed since my request. I replied in the affirmative and eventually received over a hundred pages, mostly blacked out by a censor's pen. I filed an appeal to see the deleted materials as well as the twenty-four pages that had been withheld in their entirety. My appeal was denied on the grounds of national security."

"In short," Viktor said, "you didn't get information, let alone justice."

"No," John admitted, "but I got satisfaction knowing that I had stirred the bureaucratic pot. It was worth the fight."

"Hasn't our Don Quixote ever won?" Zhanna asked.

"Oh, yes. Once. Over here."

"You must be kidding," Zhanna said. "No one wins against the Russian government."

"It was a battle over ownership of my Moscow apartment," John explained. "Some might say that I crossed the line when it comes to ethical behavior. To make a long story short, I purchased the apartment from a woman whose son, studying at an American college, was given the title by his deceased grandmother. When the mother gave all of the money to her son and none to her brother, the brother went to court to nullify the sale. The mother and son apparently thought that I would cave in and come up with an extra ten thousand dollars. I balked. I told the family that by nullifying the sale of the apartment, the son's chances of getting a green card might be jeopardized. It wasn't long before another family member, who was into 'collectibles,' satisfied the greedy uncle at no additional cost to me."

"Good on you," Viktor said. "Any thoughts about how to exact post factum revenge on people who engage in character assassination for personal or financial reward? To be more specific, Ogleby and Pickle."

"Can't help you with that," John answered. "Sorry."

"I already have an idea," Viktor said with a mischievous grin like a Cheshire cat. "Perhaps you remember the arrest of that Yale professor during the Kennedy years. He worked in the U.S. Embassy in the 1940s, and at the time of his arrest he was back in Moscow doing interviews for a book. I doubt he ever forgot the sixteen days that he spent in the Lubianka prison for alleged espionage."

CHAPTER 10

After breakfast the next day, Zhanna gathered the group for a morning excursion to the Peter & Paul Fortress. Built in 1703 and located on an island in the Neva River across from the Winter Palace, its tall bell tower is a landmark that pierces the sky. At the top of its gilded spire is a weather vane with an angel on a cross. Residents believed that the angel would protect their Venice of the North, although in olden days it was blank cannon shots that warned residents of impending floods.

Once inside the Fortress, Zhanna led the group to an open square in front of a two-story, yellow stucco building. "That's our Mint, our *Monetnyi Dvor*," she said. "Look up at the eves. You'll see a remnant of our past in relief."

"The Soviet hammer and sickle," Neville said. "The emblem still seems to be in vogue. You pointed it out to us in Moscow at the river port and on a post-office building in the center of the city. I'm not surprised. They still sell posters that say Lenin lived, lives, and will live."

"Why are there surveillance cameras on the building?" Francis asked.

"Believe it or not," Zhanna replied, "coins are still minted here."

"Also in Moscow," John added, producing a handful of kopecks. "If you have good eyesight or a magnifying glass, you can see the letter 'M' under the left front hoof of the horse of St. George as he slays the dragon. On ruble coins, the mint producer is indicated under the left claw of Russia's two-headed eagle. Take a look."

After satisfying interested onlookers, John and Zhanna moved the group into the Peter & Paul Cathedral. "This is the burial place for Peter the Great and subsequent Russian tsars," John explained. "Peter's tomb is over there in the corner, near the gilded icon wall."

Surrounding the tomb was a low wrought iron fence on which there was a white plaque with Peter's name engraved in black letters. Off to the right was a vase with fresh flowers. "Unlike other tsars in the Cathedral," Zhanna said, "Peter gets fresh flowers on a daily basis."

When they moved into the Cathedral's Chapel, there was a bouquet of flowers and a family photo next to a granite marker with no iconostasis. "After the collapse of the Soviet Union, the remains of the last tsar, Nicholas II, were re-interred here," Zhanna continued. "The picture at the foot of the gravesite is a family portrait."

"From here," John said with a straight face, "we go to prison."

"You're not serious, I hope," Francis said, unaware of how the day would end.

"The Prison of Trubetsky Bastion, sometimes called the Russian Bastille," John explained, "is one of the main tourist attractions of the Peter & Paul Fortress. As I mentioned the other day, when members of Kerensky's Provisional Government were arrested in 1917 they were imprisoned in the Bastion. Dostoevsky and Trotsky also spent time here as political prisoners, as did the internationally known anarchist Kropotkin, who is buried in the Novodevichy cemetery. The Bastion was infamous." John had a little smile on his face

"You probably don't know why John is smiling," Zhanna said. "I do. Shortly after the death of Stalin, John was given a guided tour of the Fortress by a young woman who worked for Intourist. John described her to me as a warm human being with a sense of humor, not a Soviet machine."

"She took me to a cell in the Bastion," John interrupted. "And when we exited the Fortress through the Nevsky Gate, the only deepwater landing spot, she laughed and said that now I could write home and say that I had spent time in a Russian prison."

"John was fortunate," Zhanna said. "In times gone by, the Nevsky Gate was where prisoners were loaded on to boats for execution at a location further up the Neva River. A boat is waiting for us, too. But don't worry. It's time for lunch, not death."

After a buffet on the *Novikov Priboi*, Zhanna led the group back to a pier by the Winter Palace. "To round out your last full day in St. Petersburg," she said, "we are going by hydrofoil west of the city, where there are two frequently visited tourist sites, one political and one cultural. We have time only for Peterhof, the Russian Versailles, which is about an hour away."

"Is Peterhof political or cultural?" Madge asked.

"Both, actually," Zhanna replied. "When I said political, I had Kronstadt in mind. I'll let John cover that."

"Kronstadt is a naval fortress located on an island in the Gulf of Finland not far from Peterhof," John explained. "Its sailors played a major role in support of the October 1917 revolution, but by 1921 they had become disillusioned and were demanding reforms. Trotsky, the War Commissar, rejected calls for negotiation. He issued an ultimatum. Unconditional surrender or be 'shot like partridges.'

"I was reminded of Trotsky's ultimatum when President Yeltsin ordered his tanks to fire on opposition forces in the Russian White House. As reported on Radio Echo and in Western newspapers, Yeltsin and his Minister of the Interior gave orders not to take witnesses alive. The ensuing bloodshed and destruction was horrific, although it paled in comparison with what happened to the Kronstadters."

"Now it's my turn," Zhanna said. "Peterhof was the summer residence for Russian tsars. After occupation by the Nazis and liberation by the Red Army, the German-sounding name Peterhof was changed to *Petrodvorets*. Not long ago, however, it once again became Peterhof, although the surrounding town, with eighty thousand residents, remains *Petrodvorets*. After landing at the jetty, we'll walk alongside the Marine Canal up to the Grand Cascade and the Grand Palace."

"It's gorgeous," Madge marveled. "Even better than Versailles."

The group was mesmerized by the Grand Cascade's thirty-nine gilded bronze statues and seventy-five fountains. In the middle of a pond was the main attraction, a statue of Samson wrestling with the jaws of a lion. "Myth has it that Samson was granted supernatural powers by God and performed heroic feats, like the one depicted here," Zhanna remarked. "For Russians, the Samson statue symbolizes our victory over Sweden in the Battle of Poltava during the Great Northern War."

As the group navigated around the fountains leading up to the Grand Palace, John had words of advice for anyone listening. "Be careful where you step," he said with a touch of humor. "There are joke fountains, too."

"What John means," Zhanna explained, "is that if you step on a particular stone along the path you might get sprayed, lightly, by a fountain. Children love it."

At the top of the hill was the Grand Palace, its yellow and white colors blending in perfectly with the golden fountains and statues of the Grand Cascade. The interior of the Palace was spectacular. What the group first saw was an ornate ceremonial staircase flanked by gilded statues with a magnificent fresco overhead. Before ascending, they were instructed to put 'booties' over their shoes. "It's to protect the parquet floors," Zhanna said. "When we Russians enter a friend's home, the first thing we do is replace our shoes with slippers, called *tapochki,* even though not many of us have parquet floors. It's just a custom."

"A utilitarian custom," John added. "It's a prophylactic against spring mud and winter snow in our apartments. Tourists sometimes take a pair home with them as a souvenir. Or perhaps you folks would prefer a *raketa.* That's the name of a Russian watch manufactured here in the town of *Petrodvorets* in honor of Yuri Gagarin, the first cosmonaut."

When the group entered the Throne Room of the Grand Palace, the first thing that caught their attention was the exquisite parquet floor. Eyes then went to the throne at one end of the room, three steps above the parquet floor. It is a luxurious red with gold trim, a two-headed eagle, and a gold crown topped off with a small cross. Above the throne is the painting of a figure on a horse, sword in hand.

"Is that Peter the Great?" Neville asked.

"From a distance, that's what one might think," Zhanna said. "But it's actually a portrait of Catherine the Great. More about her when we get to our next stop, Chesma Hall."

On the walls of Chesma Hall were twelve large paintings depicting a stunning naval victory by Russia over Turkey in the Battle of Chesma. "The German artist had never seen an exploding ship," John said, "which led critics to say that his paintings were not realistic. That's when Catherine stepped in. She arranged for a frigate to be exploded in Italy with the German artist as an observer. It must have been quite a show."

"Reality for us," Zhanna said looking at her watch, "is that we need to leave this UNESCO World Heritage Site and return to the *Novikov Priboi* for one last meal, a farewell dinner."

When the hydrofoil reached the Winter Palace pier, Viktor was there to welcome Zhanna and her group. Next to him stood a stranger. When Neville disembarked, Viktor nodded. The stranger walked over to Neville and thrust a thick envelope into his hands. Before Neville could say a word or open the envelope, the stranger was gone. He was replaced by two men in dark suits who moved swiftly up to Neville and said that he was under arrest.

"What's going on?" Neville asked.

"Conspiracy to foment unrest in our country," the senior FSB officer replied. "The papers that you just accepted will prove that you are part of a plot to orchestrate an Orange Revolution in Russia. As the Prime Minister recently stated, opposition leaders are being paid to carry out orders from the U.S. Secretary of State. They flock to the water trough like cows."

"That's ridiculous," Neville retorted. "Anyway, you can't arrest me. I have diplomatic immunity."

The two FSB officers both shook their heads. "A retired ambassador is not beyond the reach of our law," the younger officer said.

Neville looked around for help. Having overheard the exchange, Francis was ready and willing to appoint himself arbitrator. "Can't this be resolved with a gratuity?" he asked.

"A bribe?" the older policeman questioned.

"No," Francis replied. "Let's call it a token of appreciation."

"How much appreciation?" the younger officer inquired.

"How about a hundred dollars?"

"There are two of us. How about two hundred dollars?"

Assuming that Neville would be grateful, Francis pulled out his wallet and handed two crisp hundred-dollar bills to the older officer.

"You, too, are now under arrest," the officer responded. "Recent legislation makes it a crime not only to receive but also to offer money in return for a favor. Over here we call it a bribe, not a gratuity."

By now a crowd had gathered, trying to figure out what was happening. "Just a misunderstanding," Zhanna announced. "I'll take you all back to the ship while John and my father sort things out. I'm sure that no one will miss the captain's farewell dinner."

Viktor walked up to the affronted diplomat and the astonished psychologist. "You're going to need an attorney," he said. "You're in luck. I have a friend, a distinguished Moscow attorney, who happens to be here in St. Petersburg on business. She has connections and a good track record defending foreigners, guilty or not. Her name is Tanya. She's a good-looker, too," Viktor added, looking directly at Neville.

"I don't give a shit what she looks like," Neville the womanizer said. "I just want out of this fucking country."

"Me, too," Francis said in a troubled voice. "We haven't done anything wrong."

"I'm sure that's true," John said in a reassuring voice, "but I'm afraid you'll have to go with the officers at least until morning."

"But we're supposed to fly home tomorrow. Will we miss our flight?" Francis asked.

"I'm afraid so," John answered, "but Tanya is good. Don't worry."

While the *Novikov Priboi* passengers were on their way to the airport in the morning, with a stop at the Monument to the Defenders of Leningrad, Tanya was on the telephone to Moscow. When she arrived at the police station where Neville and Francis had spent the night with burglars, prostitutes, and a murderer, her clients had puffy eyes and ashen faces. Neville's self-assurance had vanished, and Francis seemed on the verge of a psychological breakdown.

"I've got good news and bad news," Tanya began. "After talks with influential friends in Moscow, the FSB has agreed to release Francis and expel him from the country. The only condition is that he must pay a fine of five thousand dollars. Can you arrange that, Francis?"

"I can't, but my wife can."

"What about me?" Neville asked.

"That's more complicated," Tanya replied. "What were you going to do with the papers that were given to you? I was told that they were documents from opposition leaders about corruption and violations of human rights in Russia."

"I don't know what you're talking about," Neville protested. "I have no idea who the guy is who thrust the envelope into my hand. It's a setup. It reminds me of what happened to that Yale professor during the Kennedy years."

"I know about that case," Tanya replied. "I thought about it last night when I was pondering how to win your release. It triggered my third strategy."

"What were the first two?"

"You could admit your guilt and beg forgiveness. Or you could claim diminished capacity due to age and an addiction to alcohol."

"Both are out of the question," Neville fumed. "I'm not guilty of anything, and my brain works just fine. I hope your third strategy is better."

"I hope so, too," Tanya said. "When Moscow arrests an American, particularly one who used to work for the U.S. government, they usually want something in return for the American's release."

"What might that be in my case?"

"My sources don't know," Tanya answered. "But we don't have to wait for an answer from the Kremlin. I talked briefly this morning with the American Ambassador, who had not yet been informed of your arrest. We have a meeting set up for tomorrow, and I will suggest a strategy that should please both of our governments."

"What do you have in mind?" Neville asked. "I hope it's better than your first two strategies. Convince me that you're as good as Zhanna and her father say."

"As a former State Department officer, I'm sure you know better than I the details of the Jackson-Vanik legislation," Tanya prompted her client.

"Sure. It was an amendment to a trade bill under the Nixon Administration. Granting the Soviet Union a most-favored-nation trading status was made dependent upon Moscow's willingness to let Soviet Jews emigrate freely. It didn't work. The Kremlin closed the door to Jewish emigration, and American exporters lost the benefits enjoyed by their overseas competitors. The White House now wants to repeal the law."

"That's it in a nutshell," Tanya said. "But some members of the U.S. Congress oppose repealing the law because of Russia's human rights record and concern about fraud in Russian elections. That's where my third strategy comes in."

"I get it," Neville said approvingly. "Moscow wants the law repealed, and Washington will want the charges against me dropped. It might work."

"It could take weeks," Tanya added. "I was told by one FSB official that you will be flown to Moscow tomorrow. You won't be happy with the accommodations while your case is under review."

"What should I expect? You're making me nervous."

"You'll be taken to Lubyanka."

"Not the metro stop, I assume," Neville said without humor. "I assume you mean the infamous KGB prison."

"Yes, but gone are the 'cold rooms,' where naked prisoners were beaten, dosed with ice water and slowly frozen. You will, however, be interrogated on the sixth floor of the main building without reprieve. Probably three times a day. Sessions can be as short as an hour or as long as five hours. Then you'll be taken to a cell, sometimes called a box, in the adjacent prison in the courtyard. Take heart in the fact that Francis will soon be on his way home."

"Who cares about him?"

"We all do, Neville. Just grin and bear it. You'll be next, but diplomacy takes time."

When Tanya exited police headquarters, she headed for the Astoria Hotel where she would have lunch at the famous Davidov restaurant with Viktor, Zhanna, and John.

"It's my treat," Viktor said, smiling as he looked at the menu with its mouthwatering dishes. "Let's order. Then we can talk about Ogleby and Pickle."

"For starters," the waiter said, "I recommend either blini with marinated salmon or a persimmon salad with prawns, ricola & orange sauce. Then you should try our coconut soup with crab meat. As for a main dish, today's specials are a fillet of wild sea bass or chicken *pozharsky*."

When the waiter left with the group's various selections, Tanya summarized the results of her efforts. "Pickle won't be prosecuted," she began. "Russian authorities consider him a small fish in a big pond. He will be released and expelled from the country in exchange for a hefty fine. Ogleby, on the other hand, will have to wait days if not weeks before his fate is determined. After talks with the American Ambassador and our Foreign Minister, I am reasonably certain that Washington and Moscow will come to a mutually advantageous agreement. At the very least, Ogleby's release would help to reset relations between our two countries, a goal that is emphasized on both sides of the Atlantic in words if not in deeds."

"Didn't I tell you that Tanya is good?" Viktor said, turning to John. "What I didn't tell you is that Tanya was the attorney who defended Michael Rayback's wife, Claudia, when she was arrested and tried for attempting to smuggle icons out of the country. Tanya succeeded in getting a conditional conviction, what you Americans call an adjournment in contemplation of dismissal. No small achievement."

"I would like to propose a toast to Tanya," Zhanna said, raising her glass of Soviet champagne. "Legal magician and friend of the family!"

"Now it's my turn," Viktor said, raising a glass of vodka. "In memory of my dear American friend Michael Rayback, who might or might not have enjoyed the payback delivered to Neville Ogleby and Francis Pickle by a Russian who believes that to exact revenge for a friend is morally the right thing to do."

EPILOGUE

After nineteen days in prison, Neville was released. He got a hero's reception when he returned to his university, but he would never forget the trauma caused by a false accusation. As John Milton wrote in *Paradise Lost*, revenge can be sweet at first but it soon recoils on itself.

When Francis got home he couldn't concentrate and had trouble sleeping. His physician said that he was suffering from post-traumatic-stress-disorder. It would dissipate over time, he was told, but he would have difficulty treating patients in his private practice. Not wanting to be seen as incompetent, Francis decided to retire. He had always been penny-wise, pound-foolish, but he didn't have to worry about life as a retiree. He had a devoted wife with lots of money, a small portion of which had been used to pay the fine imposed on Francis by the Russian government.

Zhanna became director of a successful tourist agency. With over four million foreigners in the Russian capital every year, business is booming. Zhanna doesn't have time for a serious romance. She is, however, a social being who loves constant interaction with people.

Tanya became a legal advisor to the President, and she hopes to speed Russia's transition to democracy. She is recognized as a champion of human rights and has been effective in helping to reset relations between Russia and the United States.

Viktor continues to dabble in a multitude of business adventures, including the importation of foreign cars. He managed to deliver a BMW X6 from a plant in South Carolina to a Russian oligarch in Moscow. It was supposed to be a birthday present for the oligarch's daughter, but there were unexpected delays. Viktor got threatening telephone calls, but he shrugged them off. *Que Sera, Sera*, he once told John after a deal involving the mafia turned ugly. He told the bandits, as they are called in Russia, that killing him would not solve anything. Viktor can be as tough as nails, but he has a soft spot for family and friends. An affront against them is taken personally and never forgotten or forgiven.

John soon dropped out of the lecture circuit on ships cruising the Volga, but he has fond memories of people he met, like Peter and Madge Krukas, and places he visited. He enjoys the quietude of living alone in his Moscow apartment, and he laughs when Viktor repeatedly says that he needs 'a significant other' in his life. John's lighthearted response is always the same, "Zhanna's too young."

John is never at loose ends. Living in Russia is an adventure. He likes being challenged, and he likes helping friends. One friend is a taxi driver turned entrepreneur who lives in Siberia and wanted to develop a tourist resort on the eastern shore of Lake Baikal. The friend had heard of the U.S.-Russia Investment Fund, which had been set up with public monies from the United States in order to encourage private sector development in the Russian economy. The friend asked for John's help in preparing a business plan.

John spent months working on the project. When the proposal was turned down, a VP in the Moscow Office acknowledged that it was a good plan but told John that the amount of money requested, just shy of a million dollars, was not enough to justify the necessary oversight of the project. John was disappointed, but it hasn't prevented him from tilting at other windmills. Satisfaction for John comes as much from trying as from winning. He remains an eternal optimist, even in Russia.